# Desperate Trails

by

Mila A. Ballentine

ISBN: 978-0-9909195-0-6

PUBLISHER'S NOTE

This novel is a work of fiction told from the perspective of fictitious character experiences. The names, places, and characters are products of the author's imagination. Any resemblance to actual persons living or dead, business establishments, event, or locals is coincidental.

❦ ❦ ❦

"Into each life some rain must fall."

–Henry Wadsworth Longfellow, *The Rainy Day*

*Part One*

# The Root

*1*

Alabaster County, *Nevada—75 miles north of Stanton County*

Drew Tanner grumbled under his breath as he made his way up the hill, tears rushing from his eyes. He crossed his arms and drew in his elbows while he sparred with the air, displaying the awkward gait of a riled eight-year-old. By the time he got to the cloudy pond on the other side, the salt of his tears was ripe on his lips and snot ran from his nose. Drew sat near the edge of the pond with his arms swathing his knees and looked at the calm surface of the water. A series of crisp yodeling grunts broke the silence in the area as a hen and her ducklings waddled through the grass to the river. He observed as the mother entered the water, leaving a growing V-line with her ducklings not far behind.

Off to the far right, a pebble plopped into the water, rousting the hen and her ducklings. Nervous groans occupied the air as the hen took to flight, leaving her ducklings to fend for themselves; still his eyes stayed on the surface of the water, timing the flow of concentric rings as they rippled towards him. It was then that he noticed a reflection on the surface of the tarn; a silhouette etched in the light of the sun with the presence of an apparition, nothing more... until *she* came out of the sun's glow. And from that moment on, the place where Drew sought and found solace was forever changed.

Drew had friends, but none that his parents would approve of until after he'd met her. From that point onward, Arlene became his shadow. Mostly, he hung out with Peter, Wayland, and Brian. From the start, it was hard to tell Peter and Wayland, gangly identical twin brothers - with spiky jet-black hair apart; until Peter fell off the monkey bars and broke the radius and ulna bone in his left forearm. That day, their eyes nearly swelled in their sockets when they saw the bulge beneath his dermis. Thankfully, it didn't pierce his skin or chunks of partially digested lunches would have hurled through the air like high-pressured water gushing from fire hoses onto the scant grass beneath the monkey bar's metal framework.

Afterward, sirens filled the air as the ambulance came and carried Peter away. He had surgery to set the bone in place, but Peter didn't ease off the rough play during his recovery, so much so that two weeks later, the bones dislodged and he had to have surgery all over again. In the end, he had a cool scar resembling a centipede that distinguished him from his doppelganger.

Brian was the tallest among the group of friend. It wasn't hard for anyone to notice his flawless dark *Pompadour,* and if any of them teased him, Miss Palmer—their flamboyant teacher who resembled Lucille Ball—would complement him every now and then. Drew could bet his britches that Brian would be smiling after class was out. For some reason, all of the girls were infatuated with him, though Drew didn't understand why. His father was a widower; at least that's what he had overheard his mom say when she spoke to her friend, Patty, over the phone. His mother died during childbirth, but his father told him some cockamamie story about her dying of a weak heart. Because his dad's hair was already gray, and they weren't even in middle school yet, he cut him some slack.

The bell rang, and students hurried out into the hall, gathering as if they were cattle let out to graze. Drew made his way through the crowd on the way to the lunchroom. He cringed when a student leaving the serving area crossed paths with him, carrying a tray with a slice of pizza on it. He clenched his eyes for a moment; *Lord knows there was nothing like a slice of half cooked pizza to get the stomach churning.* Drew made a U-turn and bumped into his friends as he was about to leave the cafeteria. They weren't keen on eating lunch either. Instead, they hustled down the hall, bursting through the gray double doors to the playground like a gang of miscreants.

Not long after they'd exited the doors to the playground, it began.

"I'm hungry," Brian's whiny voice cut through the sound of the wind.

*There is always pizza*! Drew thought as he looked at Brian, and smirked.

"I sure could use a cold drink, preferably a glass of lemonade with *lots* and *lots* of sugar." Brian picked up a rock and tossed it to the other side of the field.

"Wow!" Their eyes traveled the distance of the stone. "You should try out for baseball," Wayland said, brimming with excitement.

"No way." Brian's harsh retort cut through Wayland's enthusiasm. "I don't want to play *ball*! It gets too hot out here." An assembly line of eye rolls followed his comment.

In general, when they weren't swinging like mad chimps from the monkey bars, they congregated the way boys do, beneath shaded trees with their backs hunched and caps pulled down to their faint eyebrows. Mostly, they compared marbles or sat on the quiet merry-go-round talking about girls; not the *butt ugly* ones as Brian called them, only the ones that made their eyes gleam, the way a freshly baked apple pie sparks an involuntary urge inside to gouge the pie with your finger and shamelessly lick off the goo.

And nine times out of ten, *her* name would come up. Then, they'd go back and forth, bickering about who was cuter, Arlene McQuillen or Tammy Bromfield, a tall stringy-haired girl with blue-gray eyes the size of bottle caps. Tammy was the only other girl in their class that made them forget what they were about to say when she looked their way. Drew stayed quiet every time that question popped up and honed his listening skills instead. Thankfully, that day they had other things on their minds.

Drew broke away from the group and strode across the lawn to the far side of the playground. They trailed him. He sat beneath a chestnut oak tree and glanced blankly out at the scenery ahead. When Drew saw the look on Peter's face, he knew what was coming next.

"Whoever wins this race will do the dare!" Peter bellowed.

Peter was always coming up with wild ideas that were sure to end badly, oftentimes with them writing ten pages of lines; '*I will not do _____*' a thousand times. They got antsy after he made the declaration. Drew hoped it wasn't anything serious enough that they'd be grounded until dogs flew, pigs barked, and flamingoes slow danced to "Moon River" sung by Andy Williams.

Peter looked to the left and then to the right of him, with one eye narrowed and his lip scrunched as they circled each other.

"Quit goofing around and line up," he said, quieting them and they formed a line. "On the mark, get set, ready-y-y, *go!*"

They fled like disturbed bats out of a cave, and they didn't even know what the dare was. Drew now led the race. The next thing Drew knew, Arlene came out of nowhere matching his stride, while Peter and the rest of the gang broke away from the herd in a dead heat, leaving a trail of wind behind them.

"Eat balls!" Drew roared as he fell behind.

"Yeah!" Arlene yelled, barreling ahead with all her might. "Eat a bowl full!"

Wayland and Brian slowed down once Peter reached the finish line. Drew and Arlene came to an abrupt stop, panting heavily with their hands on their knees.

"What kind of balls?" She asked, with an inquisitive look on her face, after letting out a deep breath. Drew gave her a weird look, and then a heckling laugh erupted that brought tears to his eyes.

## 2

Overall, they were the kind of friends that one only encounters during childhood and Drew couldn't help but be amused by them, but by the time they reached junior high, they grew apart. The twins got more daring as they went through puberty, which amounted to them acting like complete hooligans most of the time. That being the case, by the time they were in high school, Peter and Wayland had a page full of juvenile offenses. As if that weren't enough, they decided to rob a convenience store in town and beat the cashier with a gun after he tried to stop them. The fact that they were only sixteen at the time was outweighed by the seriousness of their crime. They were tried as adults and were sentenced to five years for robbery with a deadly weapon. Certainly, it could have been worse; the judge gave them a lighter sentence.

Peter's first year behind bars went by without a hitch. Prison was the last place he expected to live comfortably, especially with only the bare minimum as accommodations, but he'd fared well thus far. By the second year, his good behavior afforded him the opportunity to work; cleaning certain areas. It beat being stuck in his cell or going outside in the yard and trying to remain anonymous around weight lifting, hardcore criminals.

A week into his job assignment, Peter reported to the laundry room, pushing an industrial mop bucket to the other end, and mopped his way to the middle of the room towards the double doors. Within a short time, the door squeaked as it swung inward.

"The floor's wet. You might want to come back later," Peter said as he turned to see Leon and Rolando. Leon, the leader of the duo was a bulky guy, and he'd been keeping an eye on Peter for the past few weeks when they were out in the yard, while Rolando stood aside in a seemingly nonthreatening manner, but still gave off a creepy vibe.

"Did you need to get something from the dryer?"

"No. We're here to see you. I've been watching you; you're a loner. In a place like this, you'll need friends," he said as he came up behind him. Leon put his hand on Peter's shoulders and proceeded to massage them.

"Get your hands off me. I can take care of myself." Peter grabbed Leon's hand and tried to pry it off, but Leon grabbed and twisted Peter's hand behind his back. Peter buckled, kneeing the bucket, splashing water on the floor.

"That sounds commendable," Leon said grinding his teeth as he applied more pressure to his arm. "But loners don't last long in here and besides, I can take care of you in a way that you can't."

Peter wrestled his way out of Leon's grasp and was able to put some distance between him and Leon.

"Get away from me, you sick bastard," Peter yelled.

All the while, Rolando stood there with a chilling grin on his face with folded arms. Leon rushed toward Peter, knocking him off his feet. They tumbled to the floor and threw punches back and forth until Peter broke away, making a run for the door. That's when Rolando put his foot out, tripped and grabbed Peter, slamming him against the concrete wall. From then on, they took turns beating Peter. After they'd beaten him to a pulp, they left him slumped over on the folding table.

"Now that you've calmed down, we can have a sensible conversation." Leon put his lips to Peter's bloody ear, "I want you, I want you *bad,* and I'm going to have you," he said, ripping Peter's jumper from the center of his collar down to his waist. "Just relax. Don't make this any harder than it has to be."

"Speak for yourself! I'm planning on making it real hard," Rolando said. "In fact, I'm hard right now."

After the altercation, Peter's face was swollen beyond recognition and he got sixteen stitches to repair tearing of the upper anal cavity. For the entire two weeks that he spent recovering in the infirmary, Peter didn't say a word. He just stared ominously at the ceiling with moist eyes, and yet not a single tear fell. When he was well enough, he was returned to the cellblock. A few hours after he returned to his unit, Peter was found dangling from a fixture in his cell.

# 3

Many things had changed over the years, while others stayed the same. Dwight's fist came out of nowhere and pummeled the side of Drew's jawline, leaving a bruised imprint with a left and then landed a right hook that knocked Drew off the bench he was sitting on. Spurts of blood flew from the corner of his mouth, specking the floorboards as his neck angled. Drew tumbled to the floor, bruising his face further as he landed on the porch's planked wood floor stunning him into stillness, while the wind stirred threads of the short curls of his choppy golden brown hair. As the brunt of the fall set in, Drew's light-blue eyes dilated and a line of blood traveled down his cheek and fell, leaving a spot on the wood beneath his face.

Daisy's high-pitched neighs filled the air, adding to the tension as the sorrel-colored mare eagerly bared her teeth, and tugged at the strap that bound her to the post near the steps. She stomped as she swished her sleek brown tail and kicked up a swirl of dust behind her with Drew's image mirrored in her wild eyes.

At that moment, Dwight crouched in front of him, gripping Drew's shirt into his fist, donning a merciless grin. "Come on. We've got work to do, you lazy bastard!" A whiff of alcohol scented the air as he spoke.

Sweat ran down Dwight's fleshy forehead saturating his unevenly tanned complexion; his forehead rippled, drawing attention to his disheveled, receding brown hair. Drew's eyes narrowed as he reached for the railing and stood up.

"You didn't need to hit me," Drew suggested with a rustic grit to his voice, loud enough for it to travel some distance.

"You don't get to tell me what to do—"

Dwight jabbed Drew in the chest with his index finger. Drew backed away with each jab. It was as if Dwight were pressing an ante meter. Could he recall a time when Dwight was ever nice to him? Probably not; besides, Drew figured the day that happened, pigs would do their own housekeeping. Even though he was twelve days shy of his eighteenth birthday, he was still dealing with Dwight and his rage, but he'd had enough. He wasn't the gangly boy that Dwight used to push around. He was older now with a medium-built man's physique and physically fit.

Drew charged Dwight and knocked him into the chair and Dwight stumbled to the floor. His fist grazed Dwight's 5'o clock stubble and struck his nose, drawing blood, but Dwight quickly retaliated by kneeing Drew in the groin. Drew keeled over and fell to the floor. He settled into a fetal position, grimacing as he moaned.

"I've had just about enough of you. I gave you a home, fed you, put a few dollars in your pocket and this is how you repay me?" Dwight touched his nose, looked at the blood on his hand, and then kicked Drew's side. "You should be thankful that I didn't tie your ass up in the barn and feed you through a slot."

At that moment, a two-by-four plank connected with the back of Dwight's shoulder, sending him buckling sideways.

"Get off him, you big bully! I'm going to tell my dad!" Arlene yelled as her dark tresses traced inarticulate signatures in the wind.

She advanced, dragging a hefty length of timber with one hand, the other on her hip as she closed in on Dwight. He looked up and saw Arlene standing there in a white T-shirt with the phrase *Let's Get Physical* written on it at her bust line, his eyes lowered, trailing to the pair of stonewashed, cut off shorts fraying at the edge.

"And he's going to come over here and *Kick— Your—Ass*!" She said, putting all of her *respect your elders* training aside.

It was a troubling thing for a young woman to say to a grown man, even under these circumstances. Either way, it wasn't what you'd expect to come out of the mouth of a five-foot three-inch pint size girl, but anyone who knew Arlene, knew that she had bark and a whole lot of bite to back it up.

Arlene and Dwight shared an intense stare while his lips tightened.

"Get off my property, you crazy bitch!" Dwight scowled through each word that he yelled awkwardly from the floor.

"Come on, Drew. Lucifer needs some time to himself."

Arlene helped him to his feet, placed his arm around her shoulder, and traveled down the stairs to the lawn with him. This wasn't the first time she'd come to his rescue, but he hoped it would be the last. Arlene stopped, and looked over her shoulder at Dwight lying on the porch, ogling him with her dusky-brown eyes. On the outside, the Tanner's beige home, capped by a red roof was visually appealing, a place anyone would love to call home, but that was far from the truth.

"The next time you put your hands on him, the back end of a two-by-four will be a kind gesture compared to what I'll have in store for you," she said with a grimace.

She looked ahead and they went down the stairs with Arlene feeling the weight of his arm pressing against the back of her neck as she helped him along. Dwight lay there, watching them get smaller in the distance. He took a deep breath and rested his head on the floor as the edge of his button-down shirt flapped in the wind.

❦ ❦ ❦

Drew and Arlene passed a cottonwood tree on the way to her house. A gust of wind swept through the valley, causing the leaves on the tree to patter impatiently. The gust was strong enough that the tire hanging from a branch banged the stem of the tree incessantly. By the time they got to her house, his arm was smothering her neck.

Arlene lifted his arm off her shoulder, shifting his weight as she held his side. He held the railing on the stairs to the entrance of her home and sat on the step. At that time, the broad shoulders of a man in his mid-40s with a smidgen of gray lining his sideburns and speckling his beard appeared on the other side of the screen door, his strong hand pushed the door open, and he stepped out on the porch.

They turned to the sound of the squeaking screen door. "Good afternoon, Mr. McQuillen."

Arlene's dad caught a glimpse of Drew's face. He went over to where Drew sat on the step, crouched, and raised Drew's chin.

"What happened?" Brett asked in his trademark deep, raspy voice.

Drew's forehead rippled below his broad hairline, but remained silent. Arlene's lips curled as she folded her arms.

"Mr. Tanner hit him *again*."

"I can speak for myself?" He griped.

She looked Drew square in the eyes. For some reason when she did that, it felt as though those brown eyes of hers tapped into his soul. Arlene reached over and frayed his hair with her fingers.

"Relax. I'm only trying to help."

Brett stood, and shrugged his drooping overalls up to his waist, hooked the loose strap that had come undone and let out a deep breath.

"It's a shame. I've never seen a father treat a son this way. Dwight's out of control," Brett said and shook his head.

There was a time when Dwight and Brett were best friends but their relationship changed the moment Brett found out about the way Dwight was treating his wife and child.

"If you want, I can talk to him."

Drew had made the mistake once before and said yes, but in the end, they exchanged more blows than words. Afterward, Dwight spent two weeks in the hospital recovering from broken ribs. When he was well enough, Dwight was released from the hospital, but once he had fully recovered, the beatings started again.

"I'll be fine. Dwight looks worse than I do." Drew forced a smile, but soon grimaced when a sharp pain gripped him.

"I know that I've asked you this about a thousand times, but don't you have any family you can stay with?"

"No, my grandparents on both sides passed away years ago." Drew looked away as he felt tears gathering in his eyes, but one slid off his eyelid and flowed down the side of his cheek.

Brett shook his head. "You're welcome to spend the night. I'll take you home in the morning."

"Thanks, Mr. McQuillen." Drew nodded and then sighed.

Brett went inside the house, leaving the screen door to close slowly behind him. Arlene leaned against Drew, rested her head on his shoulder, and put her arm around him.

"I'm sorry you have to go through this."

He let out a deep breath. "Me too." His lips quivered as he sat there trying not to cry.

❦ ❦ ❦

Later that evening, Drew lay on the sofa, staring up at the ceiling, while he listened to Arlene's dad locomotive snore streaming through the hall. He glanced at the wall decorated with landscape art and photos of Arlene with her parent's arm-in-arm, while the walls in his home were bare and what pictures remained of his mother were out of sight.

Rays of moonlight shone on the long hand inside the grandfather clock that cast light in his eyes and for a moment, he could swear that he saw his mother smiling at him and his heart sunk. Since she'd passed, a lot had changed, and yet life at home remained the same. Surely, there was a written law somewhere that mothers are supposed to protect their children. If not, there should be. But then again, Dwight's rampage wasn't only toward Drew, Miranda also had her fair share.

Even though his mind was churning over the ills he'd faced, Drew eventually fell asleep. He woke hours later to Arlene's cold palm touching his cheek.

"Rise and shine."

She came into focus as his eyes opened. Drew propped his upper body up on his elbows and shielded his eyes from the sun's rays.

"Is it morning already?"

"Yes. I made you breakfast. Here, this is for you." She put a packaged toothbrush on his chest. "Halitosis has been known to ruin friendships, so brush your teeth." Arlene grinned and left his side.

Later he joined her at the dining table, eating the scrambled eggs and sausage she'd made. When he was through, he looked up at her; she'd been watching him eat as she sat across the table.

"Where's your mom?" He asked after he swallowed.

"She's working the breakfast shift." Arlene took his plate. "My dad will take you home as soon as he's done shoeing the horse."

Drew's face soured. Arlene slanted her head as she looked at him. "You don't want to go home, do you?"

"Would you, if you lived with *him*?"

"No. You couldn't pay me to live with that loon, but it's the only home you've got." Arlene went to him, and put her hand on his. "You'll have to make do for now."

"I'm going to put my shoes on."

Drew stood up. He grabbed his boots, carried them out to the porch, and put them on. Arlene's body occupied the space in the open screen door and she watched while he tied his shoes. It was then that she saw her father walking toward the house and ambling up the steps to the porch.

"Good morning," Drew said.

"I'll let you know how *good* it is once it's over. Are you ready?"

"Yes." Drew stood up and adjusted his pants.

"Come on then." Brett raised his cap, scratched the thinning hair at the center of his head, and chucked the cap back down.

Arlene came out on the porch, and put her back against the railing. "I'll see you later," she said and waved.

❦ ❦ ❦

Shortly after he'd left their yard, Brett parked in the Tanner's yard. He sighed as he gazed at the house ahead on an incline with a variety of rosebushes growing around the foundation of the porch and climbing the white rose trellis. Just then, Dwight jogged down the steps, buttoning his uniform shirt, and put on a sheriff deputy's hat. Brett stepped out of the truck and met him halfway.

"You'll have to excuse me," Dwight said.

He fastened his belt, but kept Brett's muscular arms bursting out of the sleeveless shirt in the corner of his eye. When he took into consideration Brett's six-foot two-inch stature compared to his five-foot seven-inches, he decided to keep his cool and continued to the squad car parked next to his personal vehicle.

"I'm on my way out."

"What I have to say won't take long. Drew spent the night at my place." Brett put his hand on Dwight's shoulder. "Now, look here, I am not going to tell you how to raise your son, but resorting to violence won't solve anything." Brett looked back at Drew sitting in his vehicle and then at Dwight. "Is everything going to be okay between you two?"

"If he'd do as he's told, life would be grand."

Dwight pulled the door handle and sat in the squad car. Drew sat watching them from the safety of Brett's truck. He waited until Dwight drove out of the yard before he stepped out.

"Thanks for the ride."

Brett placed a hand on Drew's shoulder. "I'm happy to help, but my house isn't an inn. Now go on, and try not to upset your father," he said, as if it was easy, but Drew knew better. He climbed the stairs, turned, and waved solemnly as Mr. McQuillen drove out of the yard.

❧ ❧ ❧

Drew had a few hours to himself—hours free of his father's control. Later that afternoon he went back to finish the work he started the day before. Halfway through the task, thin splinters of hay clung to Drew's forearms and throughout his hair as he tossed bales of hay onto the barn floor. When he was through, he sat on the open tailgate and leaned back on one of the bales. After he'd rested a bit, he stacked the bales at the designated spot on the side of the barn, and then parked the truck. By then, he was drenched in sweat, so he went indoors and showered.

As nightfall neared, Drew ventured north of his house to the peak of the hill. Skit ran to the pond below and sat near the water's edge. A light breeze traveled through the prairie, tickling his hair with each flow, while it rippled the surface of the water. Nearby, ducks craned their necks and jabbed their bills into the base of their feathers and one of them waddled over to Drew stopping beside him. He watched as the duck settled in the grass, giving him the opportunity to admire its brown feathers trimmed in beige and blue.

"Hi, Drew."

He turned to the sound of the voice. "Hi," he responded in a low voice.

"You're awfully quiet today." Arlene came to him and lowered her gaze.

"It's been a peaceful day."

He looked vaguely out on the water, and Arlene glanced at him as she stood there, eyeing the pronounced brow, smooth eyebrows, the tall bridge of his nose, and narrow chin. Even when he was in a good mood, Drew always had a reflective look etched on his face—an aura that likened to an unsolved puzzle waiting to be solved—but today Arlene felt as though he was more withdrawn than usual.

She sat next to him and playfully nudged his shoulder.

"What's on your mind?"

"Stuff—"

"Like what?"

Drew looked at her. "Your parent's—they love you." He sighed. "There isn't a day that goes by that I don't feel like my dad hates me. It can't get any worse than that." Drew leaned back, supporting the weight of his upper body on his elbows and looked off to the side.

"My parent's love me and treat me well, but to be fair, you should know that my dad can be quite unruly when I don't do my chores. Besides that, I am probably the only kid in this town who has a mother that can't cook meatloaf, even if it was to save her life. Now, your mom's meatloaf was absolutely delicious," she said.

Arlene focused on a dandelion at her right side; she plucked it from the meadow, smelled it, and slipped the flower behind her ear.

Drew smiled as he looked at her, something she'd seen little of the past few weeks, but Arlene had a way of lightening his mood.

"You're right. Miranda was a good cook. She made the best sweet potato pies, too." His voice cracked a bit. "I miss her smile and the hearty way she laughed. When she was around, I mattered. I felt loved."

Arlene stood up and rested her hand on her hip. "I love you. You matter to me," she said matter-of-factly. "You're my best friend and I want you to be happy."

She wiped a tear from his eye that was about to fall, hugged him from the side, and kissed his cheek. Drew's eyes dilated and suddenly he felt as though a flock of birds was fluttering their wings against the wall of his stomach.

"Why did you do that?"

Arlene loosened her hold on him. "Because …" her eyes went from left to right, "… I can get away with it! That's why." She looked on as Drew's cheeks reddened and she giggled with her hands over her mouth.

*4*

The days blurred after that day at the pond, and before long, two weeks had gone by. By all accounts, everything was going as well as one could expect between Drew and Dwight, which lessened his anxiety, but it gave him ample time to dwell on the fact that Arlene kissed him. If he didn't know any better, he'd think she was trying to distract him, but that kiss, that sweet, soft kiss that she so readily planted on his cheek brought emotions to the surface that made his heart pace like a scared colt in a thunderstorm.

Despite his pubescent musings, there was plenty of work to do. In fact, he and Dwight spent the earlier part of the day clearing the field. As it got later in the afternoon, he glanced at his watch, parked the tractor, and trod heavily over to where Drew stood repairing the post and rail fence.

"Here. It's about that time for me to go to work." He gave Drew the spare keys to the truck. "Transfer the bales to the barn when you're through." Even in a tired state, Dwight's stern voice came across harsh.

"Yes, sir." Drew watched as Dwight made short strides to the truck, got in, and drove away.

Drew went back to fixing the fence. Afterward, he began the long trudge through the frayed grass to the house, brought the truck back to the field, and transported the load to the barn. He spent the next hour removing the bales from the bed of the truck, and when he was finished, he stepped down from the tailgate. The moment his feet touched down on the barn's floor, a swift whirring sound came seconds before he was whacked in the head. He'd stepped on a fork concealed by loose hay that fell from the tailgate to the barn floor, and in return, the handle of a pitchfork propelled full throttle hitting him on the forehead, tipping him sideways into a short-lived cock-eyed daze.

There was still much to do, but the rising knot on his forehead made it difficult for him to concentrate, and it didn't help that his head throbbed as if wild horses were bucking their hoofs against his skull. Drew staggered out of the barn to the house and held on to the railing as he went up the stairs. Once he was inside, he took a bag of peas from the freezer and placed it to his forehead for a while. Minutes later, he put the peas back in the freezer and came down the hall, scratching his arm, freeing slivers of hay that were embedded in the fine hairs on his forearm. Drew undressed as he entered the bathroom. His clothes fell to the floor seconds before he stepped into the flow coming from the showerhead, allowing the cool water to run over his head as he lathered his body. Not long after, he stepped out, wrapped a towel around his waist, and wandered down the hall to his room feeling refreshed, but his head still hurt. He dried off, put shorts on, and lay across his bed, staying there until his eyes edged to a close.

❧ ❧ ❧

Outside, an old basset hound made his way up to the porch, his under-belly dragging on each step; he lay down on his stomach, causing his gut to puff out at the sides. His portly stomach enveloped his short stubby legs, tilting them upward. He wasn't even their dog, but no one else claimed him. The dog started coming around about a year or two ago, before Miranda died. They tried luring him off the property with food, but the ole hound dog kept coming back. After a while, he grew on Miranda, so she named him *Muffin*. From then on, she put a bowl of food out on the porch. Strangely enough, Muffin would wait until they weren't around to eat, and when he was through, he'd lay there like he owned the place.

Inside, Drew lay in restful slumber in his room, while Muffin raised his head when he saw headlights coming into the yard. Dwight parked a few feet away from the porch, cut the lights off and stepped out of the car. His silhouette, albeit a dark one, filled Muffin's egg-shaped eyes. He looked up as Dwight approached the door. Muffin lowered his head as he opened the screen door. Dwight searched blindly for the keyhole, entered, and turned on the porch light and the lamp near the door.

Dwight shook his head and disappeared into the kitchen. He poured himself a glass of ice tea, removed his gun from the holster and placed it on the counter. Dwight was about to go down the hall, but instead went outside and trekked across the lawn to the barn. His stance stiffened in the doorway and he placed his hands at his waist. Dwight's face reddened as his eyes traveled the space. He shook his head and went back to the house, walked up the steps and entered the house.

He went to Drew's room and saw him sprawled across the bed. Dwight made quick strides to the bed, grabbed Drew's ankles and yanked him off the bed and onto the floor. Drew's eyes flew open seconds before his chin hit the ceramic tiled floor with a wham that made his eye tooth puncture his tongue, drawing blood. He anxiously looked around the room trying the make sense of the sudden pain. His groans quickly morphed into full-fledged bawling. He turned to see Dwight standing at the footboard.

"What did I do?" He cried through his words.

"The porch light is off, the house is dark, and if that wasn't enough, the barn is a mess. Get up!" He grabbed Drew's upper arm pulling him up to a standing position. "I'm tired of cleaning up your messes."

Venomous spittle sprayed from Dwight's mouth as he hollered. "You're useless—a waste of sperm if you ask me."

Tears filled Drew's eyes, and his jaw trembled as his emotions unraveled. He got up and charged ahead, colliding with Dwight, and fell to the floor. Drew put the weight of his body on him and threw wild punches that landed on just about every angle of Dwight's grimacing face. Their eyes reddened, lips twisted, and gnashing of teeth soon followed as a vivid rage took hold that left a metallic taste in Drew's mouth.

"You're a lousy father. What kind of man beats up on his kid?" Drew yelled.

Dwight blocked a few punches that were coming his way, and pushed Drew aside.

"Shut up, you useless-pile-of-shit!"

Dwight clumsily stood up and hit Drew just below the jaw, sending him flying backwards. He landed near the foot of the bed, and hit the back of his head on the footboard, but Dwight didn't stop there, he rushed toward Drew and kicked the left side of his rib cage repeatedly.

"You should be grateful. I can count on one hand the number of men who would take care of another man's child." He put extra effort in the last kick. "You got more from me than you deserve. Pack your stuff and get the hell out of my house. You can go on down to Vernon Clevenger's house—tell him *I* sent you and that he owes me seventeen years' worth of child support."

Drew didn't budge; he just lay there with his head awkwardly cocked against the side of the footboard in a fetal position and cried. He didn't suspect a thing until Dwight spilled the beans. Before then, he thought he was just an unfortunate child that had a dad that lacked self-control and any ounce of moral decency. Dwight stood there for a while staring at him and then walked cautiously away. Drew crawled to the door and locked it. He held on to the dresser, and brought himself up to a standing position, took a duffel bag out of the closet, and proceeded to put his things inside.

Afterward, he lay on the bed, moaning, clutching the bag with his eyes on the doorknob. A tear fell from the corner of his eye down to the sheet below. If he could help it, he planned to keep his eyes open, but eventually he fell asleep.

## 5

Drew woke just before sunrise, and looked frantically around the room. He relaxed once he remembered that he'd locked the door before he fell asleep. His body ached as he sat up in bed. He lifted his shirt and looked at his side covered with purple welts, some the size of a baseball. Drew changed his clothes, put his boots on, and from the bedpost took a hand-me-down brown cowboy hat that his grandpa gave him and put it on his head.

He glanced around the room before he went over to the dresser and pulled out the bottom drawer, set it aside and removed a wooden box. Mounds of bound bills came into view once he removed the lid. He put the box in the duffel bag and zipped it. Drew peeked out into the hallway before entering, moved reluctantly down the hall to the front door, while he occasionally looked over his shoulder and stepped out on the front porch. As expected, Muffin was asleep on the porch, but as soon as the wood creaked beneath Drew's feet, Muffin opened his eyes.

"I wish I could take you with me, but you'd slow me down. Bye, Muffin." Drew let out a deep breath as he patted Muffin on the head and then trotted down the steps.

Drew looked at the sun as it rose behind a string of hills in the distance, thinking about what he should do when a thought came to mind, but first he'd have to hightail it out of there before Dwight woke up. Yet, he took his time walking down the dirt road that led him away from his misery. Thus far, each move he made triggered a burning sensation at his side, but there was no time to nurse it. For now, his goal was to get as far away from there as possible.

*6*

As he walked the lightly traveled road, Dwight's revelation echoed like a church bell, '*you can go on down to Vernon Clevenger's house*!' When he thought about it, he realized that he'd met him a few times when he went to town with his mom. Actually, Vernon didn't live too far from his current location, about four miles down the road if he was right. So, Drew went there and knocked on the front door until Vernon answered.

A slim man with bushy eyebrows and long dark hair stood inside the mouth of the door in a white vest with a wild patch of chest hair peeking out at the top and flame print boxers.

"Do you know what time it is?" Vernon didn't wait for Drew to respond. "God's sleeping at this hour! What do you want, kid?"

"I'm Miranda Tanner's son—"

"I know who you are." He spoke with a healthy dose of impudence. "Like I said, what do you want?"

"Dwight said you owe him for seventeen years' worth of child support," he hurried his words and when he was through he clenched his eyes.

"Dwight must have lost his mind. I'm not your father." Vernon slammed the door in Drew's face.

Drew turned tail and left Vernon's yard. Ever since he'd awakened, he had been walking the shoulder of the road to nowhere. There came a time when he stopped, let the bag slip from his hand and sat on it. As time passed, Drew's head lowered into his folded arms, shielding his face from the blazing sun glaring down on him. To make matters worse, his stomach began to churn.

An hour later he heard the dull hum of an engine that got increasingly louder as it came his way, and when it got closer Drew looked up to see a vintage, sky blue pickup coming down the road, backfiring every quarter of a mile until it sat idling in front of him. An older man wearing a Nevada cap peered at him from the driver's seat.

"What are you doing out here at this hour?" It was 7 AM and packing a noon heat.

"Waiting," Drew said, rolling a twig between his thumb and index finger.

"For what?" He asked.

"A ride."

"I'm going to Trepidation to drop off some hatchlings. I can give you a ride if you'd like."

The name sounded familiar. "Is that ten miles north of here?"

"That sounds about right," the driver said and nodded.

"I'll take you up on your offer." Drew stood up, grabbed his bag, and got in the truck. "Thank you."

🐣 🐣 🐣

For the next twenty minutes, he listened to the driver tell stories about the work he'd done throughout his life and the places he visited. Drew didn't mind; he preferred to listen to him instead of focusing on the hordes of chicks chirping housed in crates in the back of the truck.

Once they got to where they were going, he dropped Drew off on the main road that went through town. Drew thanked him and the old timer went on his way.

From what he could tell, Trepidation was the kind of town where tumbleweed moseyed across the road and drivers gave it the right of way.

He stood at the side of the road across the street from a diner named Good-and-Plenty. He crossed the street, entered the diner and placed his order. Shortly after, the server returned and placed a big breakfast and a cup of tea on the table. It was then that he noticed a man sitting across from him with an impressive plate of food. He looked Drew's way.

"You've got quite a shiner there. You all right?" He pointed to Drew's face.

Drew had forgotten about it until he brought it up. The man who'd given him a ride didn't mention it.

"Oh that. I'm okay."

The man nodded and went back to eating. Drew ate in a hurry, paid, and left. He stood out front near the diner's sign, with his thumb out.

Phil stuffed the last bit of his pancakes and eggs in his mouth, licked the back of his fork, and belched. "Excuse me."

47

A woman sitting on the other side of him clutching her cup scrunched her eyes as she glanced at him. His belly rubbed the edge of the Formica table trimmed with aluminum as he eased out of his seat, releasing his bulbous gut and stood. Phil adjusted the waist of his pants and stepped outside. He shifted his weight from one hip to the other as he teetered along to his big rig, climbed the stepladder, cozied into the seat crooking his legs as he settled in, and proceeded to pull out of the parking lot. He came to a stop at the stoplight ahead. While there, he noticed someone standing at the side of the road just as the light turned green. He made a left and slowed as he approached Drew standing at the roadside.

"Where're you going?" He shouted over the buzz of the engine.

"Anywhere but here," Drew yelled. At any rate, he desperately wanted to put as much distance between him and Alabaster, Nevada.

"I'm going as far as Las Vegas."

"It sounds good to me." Drew climbed up into the truck and closed the door.

"I'm Phil," he extended his hand, they shook and Drew told him his name.

Phil drove a mile down the road and turned onto the highway. It was a long ride filled with lengthy conversations. It turns out that Phil used to be a boiler operator for most of his adult life. He'd traveled to many states, mingling with people from varied lifestyles. His life took a turn for the worse when the economy went awry and as a result, he lost his job. Like most, he had a hard time finding work.

Overall, he realized that employers weren't too keen on hiring older workers. They preferred young, pliable employees—the kind of workers they could push around. It took a while, but Phil found a job working as a truck driver, traveling around the country for a major distributor.

Eight years later, he became the manager of the company, but from time to time, he still went out on the road. He learned a lot about Phil during the long ride, even though Drew didn't utter a word besides his name.

Phil arrived at his destination—Murray, a small unknown town on the outskirts of Las Vegas. Drew thanked him and contemplatively stared as Phil drove away. A flashing vacancy sign on the Back Leg Inn about twenty feet ahead caught his attention. Drew crossed the street with a weary stride to the inn and entered. Drew glanced at the grease stained beige carpet's fraying edges, arguably the trademark of a grungy low budget hotel. An older man with red balding hair sat behind the counter with his glasses down to the tip of his nose was reading a *Sports Illustrated* magazine.

Drew cleared his throat. "I'd like to rent a room."

The attendant looked up from the magazine. "How many occupants?" He asked in a nasally voice.

"One."

"That'll be forty-five dollars a night; will it be debit or credit?" He asked in a Kentucky twang.

"Cash." Drew counted off the bills and gave it to him.

The attendant swiveled his chair and removed a key from the key rack on the wall behind him, and gave the key to Drew.

"It's the last door on the left."

"Thank you." Drew left the office and headed for his room.

## 7

Weeks later, Drew entered the lobby as the manager of the inn placed a help wanted sign in the window. He expressed interest, a lengthy discussion followed and at the end of it, the manager made a proposal.

"If you can fix that air conditioner, you have the job." Drew fixed it and started work that day.

It was an easy job considering that all he had to do was repair stuff and help with the upkeep of the inn. There were times when he cleaned the rooms when Betsy, the woman from housekeeping, had a day off. When she *was* working, Betsy sat in one of the rooms for most of the day, smoking menthol Marlboros. She reminded him of Flo from the television show, Alice, minus the 'Kiss my grits' phrase.

The job at Back Leg Inn was solid, and one he held for the next two years, until a fire damaged eighty percent of the structure. The Fire Marshal's investigation revealed that the fire was suspicious. More so, it exposed that it was the result of one of the guests cooking crystal meth in their room. Unfortunately, the owner's insurance pay out wasn't enough to cover the rebuilding costs, so that was the end of the Back Leg Inn.

Considering the fact that he was far from the city, the job market in the area was less than desirable. After all, Murray was an off the map kind of town where travelers came and went, not staying long enough for it to count, just long enough to eat, relieve themselves, get gas and maybe spend the night. So, Drew packed his bag, walked to the highway exit and hitched a ride out of town in the bed of a pick-up truck.

🐞 🐞 🐞

They'd driven for a while, passing miles of undeveloped land, before Ranch-style homes took over for the next ten to fifteen miles. After that, the bright lights and gaudy buildings of the Las Vegas strip came into view, mesmerizing him with its flashing lights and décor. It was unlike anything he'd ever seen.

A knock on the back glass broke his daze. "This is as far as I go," the driver said through the open sliding glass window.

He pulled off to the side of the road. Drew climbed out and jumped down from the tailgate.

"Thank you." Drew watched as the man drove away.

He strode down the hectic sidewalk, crossing paths with beautiful women, who looked as if they'd just left a professional photo shoot, on the arms of flashy metro men, with their hairs coiffed and greased to perfection and adorned with rings and watches with bejeweled faces. It was obvious that money talked in Vegas. If he wanted to make it here, he'd need to get a job ASAP.

He reserved a room at the cheapest hotel he could find, but it was more expensive than the rate he had paid at the Back Leg Inn. At the prices he'd be paying to rent a room, he'd need a job paying more than the minimum wage. There were a lot of businesses in the area, but it didn't make the task any easier.

Before Drew knew it, a month had gone by and his money was running out. By that point, any kind of job, minimum wage or not, was better than being unemployed. Luckily, he found a job as a dishwasher in a restaurant, two weeks before he ran out of money, but it wasn't enough to afford staying at the hotel, let alone rent an apartment.

Three weeks later, he was out of cash and luck, but he wasn't keen on the situation staying that way. Drew left the hotel with his bag on his back, and roamed the streets of Las Vegas with neon lights flashing above him. He adjusted his grip on the duffel bag and looked up at a giant cowgirl sitting with her boots in the air. At that moment, Arlene came to mind and he sighed.

He went to work that day and when he got off that evening, he decided to chance the idea he had. It was a risky venture, but instead of leaving with the other workers, he backtracked, went down the hall, entered an empty storage closet, and remained quiet until the manager locked the restaurant. As he tired, he rested his head on the duffel bag and stared up at the ceiling until he fell asleep.

He woke the next day, and freshened up in the restaurant's bathroom, knowing fully well how gross that was. He later stood outside the bathroom door, staring at it for a while, while he reflected on the things he'd unintentionally taken for granted before—like a shower and a comfortable bed to sleep in. The restaurant would be open soon so he'd have to put his troubles aside and make it through the day.

Under those circumstances, Drew was tired all the time, and after some time had passed, he felt as though he was always waiting—waiting to eat, waiting for everyone to leave so he could freshen up and sleep. He went undetected for about a month before the assistant manager arrived earlier than expected one day and found him out. Drew spent the next ten minutes being subjected to a long degrading speech and then the manager gave him the boot. He left the restaurant feeling like his gumption had been wrung out of him in a spin cycle, and now all he could do was let his head hang low to dry. *This is just a small setback*, he told himself. *I'll be back on my feet in no time*.

*Part Two*

# The Hive

## 8

Las Vegas was never short of people or exciting occurrences no matter what an individuals' financial status was. Amid the exuberance and endless flow of cash that the city was known for, Scott massaged his shoulder and moved his neck from side to side, as he rubbed the back of his neck. He put a jacket on that adhered to his statuesque arms and left work, stepping out into the ever-blinking billboard lights illuminating the streets.

Normally, he worked nights into the early morning hours, but tonight he got sick halfway through his shift. The probability of getting sick was always high in his line of work; it was the downside of working in a place filled with people. At the hour when he got off work, which was usually 3AM, the streets were bare except for employers and their employees leaving work, or streetwalkers traversing the sidewalks, at least in that area. However, on that night, Scott came across a scruffy man at the corner wearing a hat lowered to his eyes with a cup in his hand.

"Can you spare some change?" He asked with his head tilted low.

Scott stopped long enough to drop money in the cup, and continued on his way. He wasn't far from his condo that was located in a brownstone high-rise fifteen minutes away from work. He made it to the building, took the elevator up to his floor, entered his condominium, and made his way to the bathroom. He slowly undressed and stepped into the flow of cool water.

Soon after, he emerged from the bathroom with a towel wrapped around his muscular waist that showed definitive muscles that angled at his inner hip. His six-foot two-inch stature nearly reached the height of the doorway as he walked through. He grasped his head. For some reason it felt as though it was rotating on its axis. Scott pressed his hand against the wall, tightening his abdomen, further emphasizing the rigid muscles at the sides of his rib cage. He went down the hall, entered his room and lay on his bed trembling.

His temperature rose continually into sunrise … so much so that it progressed to a full-fledged fever. Scott lay delirious in bed with the towel loosening at his waist. Derrick stuck his head inside the doorway.

"Scott? Are you all right?"

Scott didn't respond. His roommate entered and touched his forehead. "Damn, you're hot—temperature-wise." Derrick sighed as he shook his head. "They said you weren't feeling well, but I didn't know it was this bad."

Derrick passed his hand on his bald dome as he left the room. He entered the kitchen, opened the refrigerator, and peered inside. The light emphasized subtle freckles on his face as he grabbed a water bottle, poured a glass, and took it back to the room.

The edges of Scott's tapered ash-blond hair stuck to his forehead and his damp eyebrows clung to his pronounced brow, and faded into his lightly tanned complexion. Derrick lifted Scott's upper body with his Herculean arms. At the same time, Scott's towel slid from his waist, exposing the side of his bare thigh and butt.

Derrick looked away and put his towel back in place. He held Scott close, ebony against ivory, and placed the cup to his lips. Seconds later, cool water spilled from Scott's lips, snaking down the groove of his sculpted chest to his six-pack, prompting his eyes to open.

"I need you to drink." Derrick brought the cup to his lips again and this time Scott drank.

"Cheese!" was heard from the doorway.

Derrick blinked as a flash glinted in the corner of his amber eyes as he sat at the edge of the bed with Scott in his arms. Lou Chang Wu stood in the doorway with a white do-rag on his head that emphasized his full light-brown eyes, and his smooth complexion illuminated under the glow of the hallway light.

Derrick shook his head as he noticed the tank top that adhered to Lou's chest, and the baggy sweatpants he had on only made it stand out more. Lou was the shortest in the house, but when it came to physique, he was the most athletic of the trio, ripped from his neck down to his calf muscles.

"You're playing a dangerous game, Lou Chang. One of these days I'm going to kick your ass, Kung Fu style."

Lou smiled, and his dimples appeared. "Contrary to popular belief, not every Asian is a master of martial arts."

Lou Chang Wu's frozen grin irked Derrick to the core. "Whatever, Lou; just delete it or else—"

Lou Chang's bantering laugh filled the hall as he made easy strides down the hallway.

Derrick let out a deep breath. "That sneaky bastard," he mumbled.

Despite the urge to punch Lou Chang, Derrick let it slide and continued to care for Scott. A couple of aspirin and a few cool drinks later, his temperature came down and in time his eyes opened as Derrick was about to leave the room.

"Derrick—" he mumbled faintly as Derrick entered the hall; he turned, looking inside the room.

"Thank you," Scott slurred.

"You're welcome, bro." Derrick continued down the hall.

Scott moaned as he sat up in bed, tightening the towel around his waist, and got dressed. He made his way to the kitchen, and encountered the blinding light of the afternoon sun where he crossed paths with Lou Chang at the entrance to the kitchen.

"You were down for the count man, but your boy looked after you in a motherly way... hell, I even got a picture to prove it." Lou Chang bit into a sandwich he'd made, and sat at the dining table across the hall.

"I'd do the same if any of you clowns were sick." Scott shook his head and thin humorless laughter followed. He made a sandwich and sat across from Lou.

"Are you going to work tonight?" Lou asked and Scott bobbed his head.

Lou Chang sighed. "I'd stay home for a day or two if I were you. The last thing you need is to be in a crowded place."

"You're probably right, but bills don't stop coming when you're sick," Scott pointed out.
He finished his sandwich and got up from the table.

Scott wasn't feeling like himself, but his fever was gone, so later on he went to work. During his break, he ventured to the back of the building and went out through the door that led to the alley. He stood a few feet from the door, looking up at the speckled sky in the poorly lit alley, when he noticed a shadowy thin figure wrapped in a dingy blanket and sitting on a stack of flattened boxes near the garbage bin. Scott thought the person was sleeping, until he saw the head move.

"Aren't you afraid of being out here by yourself?" Scott asked.

"Aren't you? I could potentially rob or kill you." A man's voice came from under a dusty hat lowered to his brow.

"Not when I consider the fact that I can kick your ass in ten seconds flat." Scott bit an inch of the Twizzler he had in his hand as he studied the young man. "You look kind of young to be out here on your own." His eyebrows furrowed. "What are you doing out here on the streets?"

The young man stood up and came partially into the light that caught the top of his cowboy hat.

"I lost my job and ran out of money."

Scott gazed at the stars. "Don't let the bright lights fool you. This city will devour you, if you aren't careful."

The young man huffed. "I know, but I'm a tough kid; country bred."

Scott extended his hand. "I'm Scott Derwin."

He stared at Scott's hand for a while and then shook it.

"I'm Drew, Drew Tanner."

## 9

"So, what's your story?" Scott asked and Drew told him the truncated version minus what his life was like in Alabaster. "It sounds like you've been through some stuff." Scott looked at him briefly and then up at the heavens. "I have to get back to work. Will you be here for much longer?"

"I guess. I don't have anywhere else to go."

Drew rested his back against the wall and secured the covers around him. Scott went back to work, but he returned an hour before closing.

"Drew," he called out, looking into the dark alley. A calico cat walked towards him, meowing and curling its body against his ankle.

"Drew, are you there?"

He saw the young man's head hanging to the left as he slept. Scott touched his shoulder and Drew's eye flew open; his hands springing up defensively, hitting Scott in the chin.

"Relax... it's Scott, from earlier."

Drew calmed down a bit. "Sorry about that, you caught me off guard."

"I live near here; you can stay at my place if you like."

"Huh—you're offering me a place to stay? What's the catch?"

"I'm just trying to give you a helping hand. You can either stay on the streets or stay at my place. It's up to you."

*He could be a pervert or serial killer trying to get me back to his place to do God knows what with me.* However, Scott didn't seem like the type, but then again, you never know. Some people are good at hiding their ulterior motives. Las Vegas was a betting town, a place where people took chances every day and it seemed like his life was as good of a wager as any other.

Drew stood up. "I'd like to take you up on that offer."

They cut through the alley to the main strip and walked the five blocks to his condominium. Within a short time, they were at the condo, taking the elevator up to Scott's floor and entered his apartment.

By the looks of it, Scott's place wasn't furnished with pricy items. Most of the furniture came from Ikea, so everything had a simplistic, but homey feel to it, especially the gray sofa and matching chairs that were arguably the best pieces in the house. Even though they gathered lint like sheep, they were comfortable. Besides that, the taupe blinds made it look like a hotel that happened to be an immaculate bachelor pad.

❦ ❦ ❦

Not long after, Derrick and Lou Chang Wu came home, filling the hall with their voices. By then, Drew had rinsed a month's worth of grime from his skin and put on the clothing Scott loaned him until his clothes dried.

"There you are." Derrick entered the living room. "Chip mentioned that you left early."

"I had to take care of something. I was starting to wonder where you guys were," Scott said.

Derrick looked at Drew, who was sitting on the chair opposite Scott in the room.

"This is Drew Tanner. He'll be staying with us for a while."

"Jeez. Some people hoard items, but you hoard people." Derrick left the living room, entered the kitchen, and opened the refrigerator.

"Where did all the food go?" Derrick yelled from the kitchen, and spun around. "You mean to tell me that you let that bottom feeder eat all of our food?"

"Bob Marley was right. A hungry man is an angry man. You'll have to excuse Derrick; he's usually not this grumpy. This is Lou Chang Wu."

"It's nice to meet you. Don't mind Derrick. He's just mad that he'll have to share Scott with yet another dude," Lou said as they shook hands.

"It's nice to meet you too." Drew came out of the living room and traveled across the hall to the laundry room.

Scott went to the kitchen. "He's not a bottom feeder."

"Come on *D*— don't you remember what it feels like to be hungry? Give the young man a break. He's a human being, no better or worse than you or I."

Derrick sighed. "I'm sorry," he put his hands up, surrendering his fight in the matter. "I lost my cool. I'm sorry."

Derrick rubbed his head fervently with one hand and left the kitchen. Scott entered the hall, made a left, and entered the laundry room.

"I'm sorry about that. Derrick can be hot headed at times."

Drew's shoulders lowered as he sighed. "It's fine, really. My *shame meter* broke the day I ate a sandwich someone had tossed in the trash."

Scott clenched his eyes as the scene materialized in his mind. "There's no shame in trying to survive. Just get your life in order." He patted Drew on the back. "Your clothes should be dry by now. I set up a cot in here across from the drier. You can sleep here until I make other arrangements."

"Thank you," Drew said, still taken aback by Scott's gesture. "I can't remember the last time someone was kind to me."

"I'm just glad that I could help. I'll see you in the morning, good night."

Scott continued down the hall to his room. Drew sat on the cot and lay down. Scott made a U-turn, came back to the laundry room and stuck his head in the doorway.

"Drew."

Drew looked up from where he laid. "Huh?"

"I might be able to get you a job. Our sweeper quit tonight, I'll even put in a good word for you."

"Thanks."

"You're welcome. All right, I'm going to bed." Scott went down the hall and turned off the light near the living room.

❦ ❦ ❦

Drew lay there looking up at the ceiling until he fell asleep. He could have easily slept until well into the afternoon, but noise coming from the hall woke him. He ventured down the hall and glanced up at the clock on the wall. If the short hand was keeping good time, it was 8AM. Come to think of it, he couldn't remember the last time he'd slept that long or awakened at that hour. He entered the dining room.

"Did you sleep well?" Scott asked.

He turned to Scott, who was eating breakfast at the table.

"Yes, it's the best sleep I've had in... three months."

"That's a long time. You can have some cereal if you want."

Drew grabbed the cereal box from the counter, took a bowl from the dish rack, and prepared a bowl of cereal. He sat next to Scott and reached for the carton of milk.

"Can you tell me more about that job you mentioned last night?"

"The sweeper job?"

Drew's eyebrows furrowed.

"You won't be sweeping floors..." he clarified. "You'll be picking stuff up."

"It sounds easy."

"I suppose so. Remember, I'm vouching for you, so do your best."

"I will. Thanks again."

❦ ❦ ❦

Drew didn't see Lou Chang Wu or Derrick for most of that day until later that evening when they were about to leave for work. Lou and Derrick walked ahead, chatting as they made their way down the sidewalk with Drew and Scott a few feet behind them.

Scott glanced at him briefly as they walked. "Are you up for the challenge?"

"I've been picking up stuff all my life, so yeah, I'm ready."

Scott nodded. "Don't let me down."

"I won't."

They walked up to the club's entrance and entered below Chip's Hunks flashing neon sign.

"Come on," he said traveling down the hall. "I want you to meet someone." They went to the office; Scott knocked on the open door, and they entered. "This is Drew, the guy that I mentioned last night." Scott turned to Drew, "Chip will show you the ropes."

Drew noticed the crooked toupee on Chip's head as he sat behind his desk with a polo shirt rimming the folds of flesh spilling over the sides of his chair. Scott

73

patted Drew on the back, left the office, and went to the locker room.

"You have the easiest job in here. All you have to do is keep the stage clean." Chip put his short stubby hands on the desk. "Stay out of the spotlight and clean as you go. It's as simple as that. Do you have any questions?"

"No, it seems simple enough."

Chip reached under his desk and gave Drew a bucket. "You're free to go then."

## 10

Drew left Chip's office, followed the music down the hall and entered a large room with colorful rotating lights that reflected their hues on the surface of the wall and on the faces of the handful of people moving around the dimly lit room. It was the first time Drew had ever seen the inside of a club, so he stood on the sidelines and took it all in.

Music streamed from large speakers stationed at the four corners of the room making the fabricated walls tremble. Women dressed in all manner of clothing kept the bartender busy delivering stellar drinks in quick succession, increasing the chatter in the room while they shimmied with their drinks in hand. Having a conversation was damn near impossible, and even with the best efforts it often resulted in shouting near the person's ear.

DJ Tryst, a highly tanned man in his late 40s with a Kangol hat on his head, sat in an enclosed booth. He changed the music, and in turn, it altered the mood in the room as it released a hypnotic beat from the surround sound speakers.

"Let's give a warm titillating welcome to Nubian Python."

His deep voice meshed with the vibrating rhythm, exciting partygoers seated near the stage and around the high-rise tables at the outer edges of the room. Derrick stepped out onto the stage as "Skin" by Rhianna came on; a seductive beat was released across the room and then Rhianna's sultry voice joined the rhythm.

The sensual melody played as the lights overhead emphasized Nubian Python's bald head. Aviator glasses shielded his eyes. He trailed his index finger along the top of the frame, then took them off and tossed them aside. He flexed into a body builder pose, tightening the custom black mesh tank top covering his torso and Lycra pants that clung to his muscular glutes. As he posed, they got a view of his pants that had a zipper at the center with openings on both sides of his thighs connected by thin chains.

He moved to the beat, while adding sex appeal to the lyrics with each thrust and swivel of his hips.

Nubian moved his muscular figure in a serpentine fashion. He dipped his sculpted upper body sending shockwaves out to the crowd. Indeed, he was hard at work and he had sweat traveling down the indentations of his chest as his pecs quivered to prove it. He rose and fell continuously like a cresting wave as if he were making love to an imaginary being beneath him and it changed the temperature in the room.

As his performance went on, feigning revelers in the audience no longer saw him as a man. His rich skin tone reminded them of sweet chocolate that they were more than eager to sample. It was then he noticed a tall, brown-haired woman making her way onto the stage in a skintight strapless red dress, balancing her frame on a pair of four-inch studded stilettos. She stood at the side, and dealt singles like a card dealer. Bills rained from her sliding hand and floated to the floor. When she ran out of money, she left the stage.

Without delay, Derrick tore his shirt off and tossed it aside. Now that his chest was bare, a collective gasp came from the crowd as he stole their breaths away. Once they regained their senses, they began to scream like wildebeests and he hadn't even taken his pants off yet.

Nubian Python moved to the edge of the stage, brought his hand over his head and motioned his body towards the crowd, lowering his hand to the zipper and pulled it down, a sight that brought many in the audience to the point of shameless anonymity.

He turned his back to the crowd, showing them his muscular back and slowly slid his pants down, beguiling the crowd as he looked over his shoulder. Surely, there were many who wanted to run their hands across the broad shoulders that were beyond their reach while he flexed his arms and body to the beat.

It was hard to take their eyes off him once he had them under his spell. Every thrust and grind of his hips was a methodical strategy to garner bills.

He worked one end of the stage to the next, while another woman stepped onto the stage. The back of her auburn hair glistened as the spotlight hit her. A blue lace trimmed bustier pressed her 36 DD's together, and the skinny jeans she wore coated her muscular thighs like a second skin.

She stepped to him, traced her index finger down the center of his damp chest, put her finger inside her mouth and tasted him. Then she pulled a twenty-dollar bill from her bosom, tucked it into his waistline and she left the stage.

All along, Drew was standing at the side of the stage with his jaw agape and the bucket in his hand. When he envisioned keeping the stage clean, it didn't involve picking up stripper tips.

Chip came up behind Drew. "What are you waiting for? Clean the stage," he said, and gave Drew a nudge.

## 11

Drew looked out at the crowd, cheering wildly, and then looked down at the money covering the floor. He came on stage and avoided the spotlight as he cleaned the floor. He had cleared the stage and the front row by the time Nubian Python left the stage and went back behind the curtain; Drew was emitting a cold sweat as an intermission of pop music came on.

"Are you okay? You look flushed," Chip asked.

"I'm fine."

"Go and empty the bucket in the tray with the dancer's name on it and come back. Hurry up, the next act is about to come on."

Shortly after, DJ Tryst lowered the music and his voice cut in. "Ladies!" DJ Tryst prolonged the "s". "Let's give a warm welcome to Great Scott," he said as if he was introducing a contender for a boxing fight.

Great Scott emerged in lieu of low bagpipes that slowly meshed into a full-fledged Dubstep beat, and as the spotlight expanded it revealed his Schwarzenegger build and a shredded kilt that went down to his knees, drawing attention to his taut calf muscles. Scott swayed his hips, moving his center forward as he danced provocatively to the left, right, and center of the stage. At that point, he tore off his shirt, releasing captive eight-packs that were hidden underneath, and revealed his nipple rings that glinted under the strobe lights.

Great Scott ran his hands through his ash-colored hair, and lowered them to his chest, sliding them down to his waist. He flipped into a handstand, and the kilt came down to his chest, revealing what arguably lies beneath every Scottish man's kilt, sheer nylon underwear with an opening at the front where a silk sock covered his manhood with the Scottish flag at the tip.

Bills showered on the stage from every angle, falling like torrential rain. The crowd erupted in cheers that morphed into them chanting, "Great Scott, Great Scott!"

Colette and Leslie, both back-up singers, were out on the town looking for a good time on their day off and sat two rows away from the platform, pattering their feet as Great Scott heated up the stage.

"I think strippers have super powers," Colette said as she rummaged through her purse while sitting next to Leslie.

"Yes, they have the power to suck every dollar out of your wallet if you let them." Colette left Leslie's side, went on stage and waited for her opportunity.

He came out of the handstand, landing on his Timberlands and unbuttoned the kilt as he innately switched his hips and popped his booty in the sheer brief while his sleeved penis waved the Scottish flag. Colette approached him, slipped a ten into his sheer undergarment, and left the stage.

Great Scott danced for the next fifteen minutes, but to Drew it seemed like a lifetime. Scott finished his performance and left the stage. Drew came behind, picking up the bills from the stage as the DJ changed the tune to pop music that in time changed to Rap and R&B tunes.

After some time had passed, DJ Tryst intervened again. "Ladies! Our final act, Asian Persuasion is about to enter the stage. Are you ready?"

A resounding *yes* filled the room.

"This is a public service announcement. I repeat… this is a public service announcement: Tip your friendly neighborhood stripper."

Asian Persuasion came out on the stage under the spotlight that accentuated his dark tapered hair, subtle brow, vibrant brown eyes, and scrumptious lips, that on any given day a woman in the audience would trade her left nipple to kiss. His high cheekbones, angular chin, and smooth, silky skin added an exotic contrast that elevated his sex appeal. He proceeded to do what he does best—arouse the crowd.

Asian Persuasion was the last to perform that night. The crowd lessened, and they went on to prepare for closing time. An hour and a half later, Chip locked the entrance door and they walked home.

Drew hadn't said a word, so Scott initiated the conversation. "How did it go?"

Drew's jaw tightened. "Okay."

"It doesn't sound like it. If you don't like the job, you can quit."

Drew stopped. "Why didn't you tell me that you guys were strippers?"

"I didn't think that it mattered. After all, we could be doing worse things." Scott left Drew standing there and continued walking.

"I didn't mean to—I wasn't prepared for what I saw, that's all."

Scott stopped and turned to him. "If you're going to work there, you'll have to focus on what matters— making money—or else you won't last a week."

Drew rubbed his forehead. "How do I do that?"

"Just think of it as a means to an end." Scott put his hands in his pockets and continued ahead.

## 12

Now that he'd seen his roommates writhing bodies, he couldn't get the images out of his mind. Drew moved about restlessly on the cot well into the wee hours of the morning before he fell asleep.

He woke hours later, but stayed in the laundry room, despite all the busy chatter going on in the living room. Drew laid on the cot, mulling over the choices he'd made. He was grateful that Scott offered to help him, but now he wasn't sure if he'd made the right decision.

Lou Chang entered the kitchen, brushing his hair excessively. He took a small water bottle from the fridge and went back to his room. Derrick and Scott were in the living room playing Xbox. Derrick pushed the pause button on the game and went down the hall to the bathroom. He stopped when he heard music coming from Lou Chang's room, and then peeked inside.

"Dude, what are you doing?"

Lou stood at the center of his room in a sheer tank top with his back to the door, watching YouTube videos of Rain, a K-Pop idol, mimicking his hip movements.

"I'm practicing. Watch out, Nubian Python, I'm going to take your number one spot. Then, I'll be the best stripper in the house."

Lou didn't miss a beat during their conversation. Derrick shook his head as he left the doorway, and entered the bathroom.

❦ ❦ ❦

Later that evening, Jake—another dancer from the club who went by the stage name *White Stallion*—stopped by wearing a baseball cap, oversized T-shirt, and baggy pants. Under his shirt lay a fully tatted back, etched with angel's wings.

Jake and Scott exchanged a three-step handshake and then he moved on to Derrick. "Have a seat. We're playing Call of Duty. You're welcome to join us," Scott said.

Jake sat at the end of the sofa next to Scott, and Derrick was on the opposite side in the single chair.

"No thanks, but I'll watch."

Jake looked on as they played. Once they'd finished the game, the living room erupted in fervent chatter as Jake gave his verbal recollection of what took place after they'd left the club a few nights ago.

"Luke Warm went on stage. He was in the middle of his show when a woman came on the stage raining bills in the air like she had stock that had reached the prime value. Mind you, she was a big girl, and you know strippers love big girls, or as I like to say, perfectly plump ladies. Anyway, the bills floated to the floor like a feather losing wind and most of them clung to Luke's skin as he rippled his body. Then, he lifted and pinwheeled her, setting her knees on his capable shoulders, but his knees buckled and she slipped from his grasp," Jake said, and proceeded to laugh under his breath. "Do you know she had the nerve to ask for her money back? Doesn't she know that strippers don't give refunds?" Jake asked with a serious face, but they ended up laughing at his outlandish comment.

Drew was still in the laundry room. After last night, he wasn't sure he could face them with a straight face, until his tummy began to moan. Moments later, he emerged, crossed the hall, and entered the kitchen. Laughter came from the living room and echoed into the kitchen while Drew peered inside the refrigerator.

He made a sandwich, went to the dining room, and sat at the table. The dragging of the chair's legs on the surface of the tiles made a screeching sound that caught their attention in the other room.

"Drew, is that you?" Scott asked.

"Yes," he said and then bit into the sandwich.

Scott stood, and peaked in the dining room. "When you're finished, I'd like you to meet someone."

"Sure. I'm almost done." Drew scarfed down the rest of his sandwich, washed it down with what remained of his drink and went to the living room.

"I'd like you to meet Jake. He's a dancer at the club," Scott said as he stood between them. "Drew's the new sweeper."

"I knew he looked familiar. Do you like the job?"

"I like working for an honest wage," Drew said. Jake nodded as he looked at him.

"Join us. We're swapping stripper stories, not that you'd have any to share, but you might learn something," Lou Chang said with a smirk.

Drew's face bunched into an unpleasant grimace. He sat near Derrick on the loveseat.

Scott chortled. "That was a nice story, but I've got a story of my own. *Mikael Angelo*, a former stripper, put a chair on the stage. He picked a woman out of the crowd, brought her on the platform, and she sat in the seat, but not for long. Mikael lifted her, turned her body upside down, put her in a handstand and rested her knees on his strong shoulders. Thankfully, she was wearing pants, albeit short ones. He faced the crowd, so all they saw was her back even as he executed his signature moves, moving his muscular legs, propelling his center back and forth, all while making his six-pack flex. After a few minutes of her inner thighs straddling his neck and shoulders, Mikael keeled over and they both came crashing down with him landing on top of her. His legs came down on her shoulders and his crotch smothered her face." Scott paused briefly. "I bet she didn't expect to be ball and gagged that night."

Scott laughed and shook his head. "And that's not the worst part. He'd seen a portion of her *unmentionable* through the pants opening, that's why she slipped from his grasp. They both walked away from the incident slightly embarrassed but unharmed. However, it turns out that she'd sprained her back, so she filed a lawsuit against him."

"This job has advantages, but strippers have an expiration date in this business. I hope you guys have an exit plan." Jake relaxed in the chair. "How old are you?" He pointed at Derrick.

"Twenty-six."

"And you?" Jake went down the line.

"Thirty," Scott chimed in.

"Twenty-three and counting, baby," Lou blurted out.

"Now, Scott you're at that age when a stripper starts to fizzle, but you're a savvy guy, so you can probably put in two to three more years, tops. Derrick you're getting up there, so pace yourself. Don't make the same mistake that Luke did. Avoid lifting heavy machinery."

It was hard for Jake and everyone else to keep a straight face after his last remark, but they did. They sat there nodding contemplatively. Jake was making more sense than Scott cared to admit. There had to be more in his future besides stripping, and sooner or later, he'd have to figure it out.

"I appreciate the advice. I'll think about what you've said," Scott said.

"Me too," Derrick added.

"Lou, you're an ambitious guy. I can see that you're aiming for something. Although, I'm not sure what that is, but I hope it's worth the trouble. As for me," Jake eased out of the sofa, "I'm thirty-six and my stripping days are over! I'm opening a smoothie café on the boulevard at the end of the month."

Scott patted him on the back. "Congratulations." Lou and Derrick echoed the sentiment.

"I'm curious. How does one go from stripping to making smoothies?" Lou Chang asked and laughed immediately thereafter.

"Nevada is a humid place. Everyone needs something to cool them off whether it is a stripper or a smoothie. On that note, I'll be on my way. I have some errands to run."

They said their goodbyes and Scott escorted Jake to the door. Scott closed the door and rested his back against it as he looked off to the side absentmindedly.

"Are we going to finish this game?" Derrick yelled from the living room.

"Yeah! I'm coming." He sighed and went back to the living room.

🐞 🐞 🐞

They wrapped up the game and went off to do other things. Scott ventured out on the balcony, sat on the lounge chair, and looked out at the Las Vegas skyline. Derrick went to his room and lay on his bed reading.

Shortly after Scott left, Lou went to his room, and, not long after, music floated down the hall from his stereo system as he practiced his stripper moves.

Now that everything had died down, Drew was the only one left in the living room. He came out on the balcony and glanced briefly at Scott before indulging in the view ahead.

"The view is beautiful."

"You'd never think that this city has any faults by looking at this view," Scott said. He sighed and dragged his thumb and index finger along the frame of his chin repeatedly.

"I'm probably the last person you should listen to seeing that you found me in an alley, but the moment I decided that I wasn't going to allow others to dictate my journey, that was the moment when I truly began to live."

Scott nodded. He closed his eyes and listened to the muted sounds coming from below the high-rise. They stayed out there for a while, quietly savoring the cool air until it was time to get ready for work.

Ordinarily, they weren't keen on getting to work too early, but tonight everyone was eager to get out of the house. They even made quick strides and arrived at the club earlier than they usually did.

❧ ❧ ❧

Despite Jake's revelations earlier that evening, Lou remained focused. He was more determined than ever to perfect his skill. In his case, Jake had to be wrong. Lou could strip well past thirty if he wanted to and retire comfortably. He rubbed his hands together as he left the dressing room and traveled down the hallway to the stage door.

"Ladies, I know you've been waiting all night for this one. None other than Asian Persuasion is about to grace the stage. Are you ready for some sugar?"

Lou Chang stood off to the side, straightening the red bow tie on his neck as a smooth electric guitar solo blared from the surround sound speakers with a start-stop-kick drumbeat. The intro of "Pour Some Sugar On Me" by Def Leopard coursed through the audience like electric rain, wooing them as the tune spread in the room.

Asian Persuasion moved on stage, sliding into the spotlight with one leg trailing the other as his feet slid across the floor. He snapped his fingers as he came to a stop and danced his way to the center of the stage. Joe Elliot, the lead singer of Def Leopard, joined the ensemble in his edgy voice.

Asian Persuasion let the rhythm take over, flowing with it as if it was his heartbeat, while he pop-locked and danced his way into their sexual fantasies. He moved his abdomen, and stirred his body in slow motion in a pinstriped vest that put his muscled arms on parade. His pants coddled his derriere, but slackened from the thighs down to his ankles. He wasn't as bulky as the other dancers were, but he had a nice body and the ladies loved to love him.

As his act progressed, he brought a leggy woman with cinnamon hair wearing a flowing knee-length dress on stage and held her by the waist. He pulled her closer to him and lowered into a split, springing up with his hands against the side of her legs, raising the side of her dress as he came up to a standing position, then whispered in her ear.

Her petite hands held his wrist and she wrapped her legs in his. She held on tight to him and he cartwheeled her as her heartbeat ravenously in her chest. When he was through, he put her down on her own two feet, but he wasn't finished yet. He took her hand, dipped her in his arm, brought her up and then he let her go. She left the stage completely winded.

Asian Persuasion moved closer to the rod at the center of the stage, held on, raised and orbited his body inches from the pole as if he was executing flares on a pommel horse. He positioned his legs in the air, wrapped them around the pole, and inched his way up. Then, he heaved his body outward into a back flip and landed on his feet.

As soon as he landed, Asian Persuasion tugged his pants off, tossed them aside, and faced the crowd in a nude seamless brief. His bits and pieces were all on display, not to mention his noteworthy accessory covered by a penile casing slanting up to his hip and peeking out at the waistline. Not only did it have a casing, but it also had two dime sized wiggle eyes at the top that jiggled with each move that he made.

Lou spun around, unbuttoned the vest, and gave the audience a view of his chest, his perfectly cut abdomen, and his nipples that seemed to fade into his lustrous skin. He lowered into a split as the song returned to the raunchy seductive intro strung together with a start-stop beat.

Once he finished dancing, he faded into the spotlight as it dimmed. Drew came out on the stage and picked up the bills that were scattered around the stage floor and walkways, doing so after each act, every day, six days a week for the next four years.

## 13

Drew stood in the laundry room's doorway and peered inside. He saw Derrick standing off to the side ironing bills in nothing but skintight boxers and slippers, rehearsing something while he occasionally glanced at a sheet of paper. He'd seen him do it countless times before, but didn't think much of it until then.

Drew traveled down the hall to Scott's room and looked inside, but he wasn't there. He hadn't seen much of him in the last three months, except for when it was time to report to work the next day. Drew passed by Lou's room. As he came to expect, music came from Lou's room as he trained.

Drew went out on the balcony to get some fresh air and looked out at the hazy skyline as the sun lowered in the horizon. Scott came home, went out on the gallery and rested his hands on the railing. Drew looked in his direction as he sat there.

"Is everything okay?" Drew asked with the faint sound of cars rising from the streets below. "You've listened to me when I had things on my mind. The least I can do is to listen to you."

Scott looked at him, sighed, and sat beside him.

"I've lived in Las Vegas since I was sixteen. I ran away from an abusive foster home in California, and caught a bus to Las Vegas. By then, I truly believed that anywhere would be better than where I was living, but you and I both know that that's hardly ever true. A month later, I started hanging out at a YMCA. During that time, Derrick's mother signed him up for an after school program there and that's when we met and became friends. He looked up to me like a big brother. Derrick didn't know that I was homeless at the time until I showed up on his doorstep asking for food. After that, there was no way around it. I had to tell him. Derrick asked his mom if I could stay with them. She was against it at first—who could blame her? After all, I was technically a runaway, but once I explained the horrible conditions I endured in my foster home, she let me stay. Derrick saved my life, and ever since that day, I promised myself that I'd do the same for someone else. I'd like to think that I've fulfilled my promise."

Tears fell from his eyes. "Derrick's mom passed away a year after he graduated from high school. Things weren't easy for us, and in the long run we learned firsthand what it felt like to be hungry." He paused for a while before he continued. "Our finances dwindled, and we were on the verge of being evicted when I came across an ad in the back of the newspaper for male dancers. I auditioned and got the job, but we were barely able to pay the rent, let alone eat. Derrick was a freshman in college at the time, but he dropped out after he'd finished the first year. The next thing I knew, he was in the club dancing too. The best thing that's come out of what we do for a living is this condo we bought five years ago. Despite all of the progress I've made, I've been feeling down lately."

"I'm sorry you had to go through that. Now I understand why you did what you did for me. I'm grateful that you came into the alley that night. Had it been anyone else, they probably would have pretended like they didn't see me." Drew sat there looking ahead. "If anyone told me six years ago that three guys who strip for a living would make a difference in my life, I'd have said they were crazy." Now tears flowed from his eyes. "Ever since my mom died, my father treated me worse than when she was alive, but you've all gone out of your way to make me feel welcome and feel at home, so don't be so hard on yourself."

Scott nodded as he looked at his watch. "I'll try to keep that in mind. We have to be at the club in an hour."

Scott went inside and got ready for work. Derrick and Scott left the apartment, leaving Drew and Lou Chang Wu to follow minutes later. They walked to the club as Lou sang along with the music coming from his headphones. Drew touched Lou's shoulder.

He stopped, removed the headphones, and looked at Drew. "How did you and Scott meet?" He asked. They continued walking.

"I met him two years before you became the fourth wheel. I was a street performer break dancing at various locations around town. At least until the Las Vegas police started to crack down on the scene. According to them, 'we were jeopardizing the integrity of the businesses in the area.' The officer gave us a warning:

'the next time we catch you out here you'll see the inside of a jail cell.' I've been doing street performances since I was thirteen. I love dancing, but nothing is worth losing my freedom. So, I quit doing street performances. Before then, Scott saw me perform a couple of times, and always left a generous tip, so one day I approached him and struck up a conversation. I finally got around to asking him what he did for a living. He hesitated, but I persisted. I guess he thought I'd think poorly of him, but who am I to judge? I didn't give it a second thought when he told me that he was an exotic dancer. During that time, I was living at home with my parents, but unbeknownst to me, they were trying to set me up with another Korean American family's daughter." Lou rolled his eyes. "When I say that I have seen shoes cuter than her, I'm not kidding. I refused to marry her and my mother lost it. She slapped just about every part of my body that she could access. 'Babo,' she yelled. 'Fool.' I've never seen her that upset before," he said and chuckled. "After we'd become friends, Scott got an ear full of my troubles on a regular basis and occasionally he gave advice, but the situation was too much to bear. It was the worst three weeks of my life. I had to get out of there, so I asked Scott if I could rent a room at his place until I found an apartment of my own. He was okay with it, so I moved in and I've been headache free ever since."

Cars hummed as they drove by them on the way to the club. The signs on the buildings served as auras as Drew and Lou ambled along the sidewalk and talked.

"I was unemployed at the time, but I had no intention of mooching off Scott. I was born to dance, so I thought that dancing at the club was another way, albeit a freaky method, to continue doing what I love. Scott wasn't thrilled when he learned that I'd be dancing at the club. He advised me to do something else, but my mind was already made up." They walked the last block and entered the club.

🐞 🐞 🐞

That night wasn't any different for Drew than any other night. It consisted of waiting and cleaning. At the end of his shift, Chip and Drew talked off to the side as he locked up for the evening, while Scott, Lou Chang, and Derrick waited for him. After their conversation ended,

Drew jogged over to them. They left the parking lot, and halfway home, Derrick and Lou Chang started smacking one another and mimicking Matrix moves.

"Don't those two ever get tired of clowning around?" Drew asked.

"Nope. They live for that shit," Scott said.

Drew snickered. "There's something I have to say—"

"What is it?" Scott slowed his pace.

"I'm leaving. I'm going home."

Scott paused for a moment and then continued walking. "Are you sure about that?"

"I am. I'm ready."

They walked side by side, following Lou and Derrick. Deep down, Drew knew he'd have to break the news to them as well, but he wasn't looking forward to it.

## *14*

Days later, he put his duffel bag on his shoulder, retrieved his hat from the washer, and went to the living room. For the past few days, conversations were at a minimum, but once Drew stepped out into the hallway with his bag in hand, that quickly changed.

Scott went up to him. "I'm going to miss you. You have an air of innocence about you. Don't lose that. This world can be a cruel place, but there's no rule that says that you have to emulate its cruelty."

"Take care of yourself," Lou Chang said and shook his hand. Derrick shook his hand too.

Drew's eyes traveled the space he'd occupied for the last four years one last time. "Thank you. I'll never forget what you've done for me." He wiped tears from his eyes and closed the door on the way out.

Not long after, a cab dropped him off at the greyhound bus station and within the hour, he boarded the bus. He had a long ride ahead of him, a ride where he would encounter crying babies, loud salacious cell phone conversations, and people telling him their life story without even knowing his name.

Six hours later, the bus pulled into the station in Missouri, Nevada—the closest station to Alabaster. He stepped down from the bus into the blistering heat knowing that home was within reach, but he still had fifty miles to go.

Fortunately, an older model Ford, one Drew hadn't seen in his lifetime, slowed down as it came his way. The driver, donning a tan fedora, tropical shirt with green palm fronds on white and linen pants came into view. He was dressed as though he was on his way to an exotic location. Eugene, the proud owner of the vintage gas-guzzler, introduced himself. He offered Drew a ride and he gladly accepted.

"I'm eighty-nine-and-a-half," the octogenarian said unexpectedly, reminding Drew of what mothers' say when they have a young child.

Drew smiled and nodded. He glanced at a guitar lying on the seat between them. "Do you play the guitar?" He asked. If not, why else would he be traveling with the weathered instrument?

"I've been picking this here guitar since I was nine," Eugene said as his crooked fingers, grasped the steering wheel.

They were laden with wrinkles, arguably, the marks of life obtained by someone who'd lived a little, and he had the age spots to prove it. Yet, he had a light in his eyes that was wild and free.

"Do you know how to play?" Eugene briefly took his eyes off the road, glancing his way.

"A little. My mom taught me. I can play something… if that's okay with you."

"Sure, why not. Play me something with a little soul and some heartache into it."

Drew thought for a while before he reached for the neck of the guitar, put it on his lap, and strummed the strings.

"It needs to be tuned, but I can do that."

He adjusted them one by one, nodding as the note played. Immediately thereafter, a flavored, rustic melody flowed from it as he sang, "I Am a Man of Constant Sorrow" by The Soggy Bottom Boys.

Eugene joined him in the chorus as Drew played and when that song ended, they sang other songs, to the delight of Eugene who decided to take Drew all the way to Alabaster.

An hour later, Drew stepped out of the idling car and looked at Eugene. "Thank you."

"No, thank *you*. You made my heart smile."

The truck eased down the road, and just like that, Eugene and his guitar were gone.

*Part Three*

# Home

## 15

Drew hiked the bushy path through ankle-high grass, and then passed the cottonwood tree where a dilapidated tire swung lazily with a bird's nest in its hollow. He continued to the house, jogged up the steps and looked to his left, hoping to see Muffin lying there, but he wasn't. Drew moved closer to the rusty screen door hanging on one hinge, and knocked. No one answered, so he knocked again.

A coarse, rabid voice came from within the confines of the home. "Aren't you supposed to be off today?" He yelled as Drew turned the knob.

The door was open, so he entered, followed the voice down the hall and entered Dwight's room. He noticed a collection of prescription bottles next to a jewel-embezzled frame with a photo of his mother in it on the nightstand near Dwight's bed. His eyes traveled to where Dwight was lying on the bed. Dwight looked older now, his hair was almost fully gray, and there was something about him that didn't look quite right.

"Hi, Dad."

Dwight lay in bed with drool coming down the corner of his lip and there was an uneasy look in his eyes. "Dad? Who the hell are you and what are you doing in my house?" He yelled.

"It's Drew, your son."

"I don't have any children," Dwight slurred.

His comment reminded Drew of what he'd said the day before he left town. Even though many years had passed, Dwight's words were still capable of causing excruciating pain, as much as a blade laced with lime cutting through his skin. Drew balled his fist as Dwight's fighting words marinated in his head, and still, Dwight's appearance made him worry. In fact, he was certain that his face was disproportionate.

Drew walked to his bedside. "What happened to your face?"

"What's it to you?" Dwight asked with sass to his voice.

Drew tsked. "I'll be in my room, if you need anything." Drew walked to the door.

"What room? Not in this house! Get out or else I'll call the police!"

"Call them!" Drew griped and left the room.

Upon entering his room, he noticed how clean it was. For a man who didn't have a son, it was obvious that someone was keeping it clean. Drew put his duffel bag at the footboard and crashed on the bed.

❦ ❦ ❦

An hour later, Patty, Dwight's caregiver entered the home and traveled down the hall. She passed Drew's room, but backtracked when she noticed someone lying on the bed. Patty peeked inside and then she continued down the hall to Dwight's room.

"I see that you have company."

She sighed as she looked at the articles of clothing that were lying around the floor. Her layered hair and feathered bangs flared as she picked up his droppings. When she straightened her average-sized frame, short waves of light-brown hair framed her oval face.

Dwight squinted as he got a glimpse of the bright red lipstick she paired with a dark floral shirt. Patty rolled her eyes at him and pressed her full upper and thin lower lip into a frown. Despite her lack of fashion sense, when he looked at Patty's dark blue eyes and Barbie-like features, she made him forget about his condition for a while.

His eyes traveled the span of her face. "What are you talking about?"

"The man in the other room, who else would I be talking about?" Patty stood there with one hand placed firmly on the waist of her elasticized jeans.

Dwight sucked his teeth. "I told him to leave. I want him out of my house." He tried to get out of bed, but fell back onto the mattress in a pitiable manner. He thumped the mattress. "God damn it. This isn't a hotel."

"Calm down. I'll have a chat with him."

Patty walked through the hall with her shoes making a squeaking sound as they made contact with the floor. She knocked on the open door and entered.

"Rise and shine!" She spoke with a dainty, elevated voice.

Drew raised his head in acknowledgement, but it wasn't enough to satisfy Patty. She walked over to the bed, and yanked the sheet off him and tossed it aside.

"What are you doing here? And just so you know, don't think about trying anything funny; I'm packing a mini revolver that can give you something to limp about." She patted a cross shoulder bag resting on her hip.

Drew looked at her like she was crazy. "What? I'm Dwight's son, Drew."

Patty gasped, opening her mouth wide enough to swallow a toad. "Well, I'll be damned."

Drew recognized her, but he couldn't recall where he knew her from. His eyes rose and fell until they closed and his head plopped down on the pillow seconds later. Patty stood there for a while watching him sleep and then she left the room. She entered the bathroom, cringing at the sight of the hideous floral wallpaper, and turned the water on, filling the tub.

Patty turned the water off and went back to Dwight's room. "Come on, let's go."

Patty helped him up from the bed and took him down the hall. He was out of breath by the time they made it to the bathroom and sat on the closed toilet lid.

"You know the drill," she said, slightly lowering her chin as she stood there.

His hand trembled as he tried to undo his button up pajama top. She got tired of seeing him struggle and unbuttoned it for him. Dwight stared wearily at the tub filled with suds.

"Why do you always add so much soap?" He asked.

Patty was a woman settling into her mid-forties who was no longer interested in pleasing Tom, Dick, or Harry. She exhaled and placed her hands on her hips. He'd asked her that question a few times. He deserved an answer, even if he was getting on her last nerves.

"I don't want to see your balls—that's why. I might lose my lunch. Now let's get this over with!" She huffed. "Pull your pants down and I'll help you get in the tub." Dwight did as she instructed, but he was also pulling his boxers off along with it. "Not the boxers, Dwight, just your pants."

Dwight shrugged his pants off. Patty kept a close eye on him as he stepped into the tub and sat down. She washed his upper body and legs, and then gave him the rag.

"Go on. You know what to do."

Dwight took the rag, washed his privates, and extended his hand with the rag to her. Patty flinched at the sight of it. She pinched the rag out of his hand and dropped it in the sink. Patty helped him get out of the tub, wrapped the towel around him, and took him to his room. She stood aside and let him do whatever he had to do, but she pitched in when it became too cumbersome for him.

"Are you all set?" Patty asked. Dwight nodded.

"I'm fixing to go outside. Are you coming?"

"I'll stay in the living room."

❧ ❧ ❧

Drew woke and ventured out into the hall past the living room where Dwight watched TV, and went out on the porch. He saw Patty sitting in a rocking chair off to the right and walked to her.

"I know you from somewhere, but I can't recall."

"Of course you know me. I was your mom's best friend."

"That's it. I knew you looked familiar. I haven't seen you since mom died."

"I loved Miranda like a sister, but we weren't on good terms when she died. I blamed myself for the breakdown of our friendship, but I can't even remember why we stopped talking in the first place." Patty exhaled. "If she were sick beforehand, I wouldn't have taken it as hard, but she just up and died without any warning of a brain aneurism. Not that one ever gets much notice about such things. I should have been there for her, but I wasn't. That's why I didn't come around." Patty wiped a lone tear from her cheek. "I only started to come around last year after Dwight had a stroke." She looked at him. "By the way, I'm sorry for threatening you earlier."

Drew's eyes wandered as he nodded. "It's okay. I figured that you thought I was a drifter who planned to take advantage of Dwight. Actually, that's not a bad idea."

"He was in bad shape when I arrived." Patty shook her head. "It was awful. He made a grave mistake when he hurt Lucy." Patty noticed Drew's forehead rippling. "Lucy was his first caretaker. He was always barking at her but one day he took it too far. He grabbed her by the arm and sunk his nails into her skin." Patty lit a cigarette and dragged on it. "Lucy'd had enough of his abuse. She left right after it happened, leaving him with a load of poo in his adult diaper." Patty smirked, savoring the moment. "Lucy showed him! I guess he thought that every woman was going to put up with his nonsense." Patty dragged and puffed smoke before continuing. "By the time I got here, he smelled worse than trash that was steamed and rolled in a garbage truck. I had to peel a couple of loads of crusted turd off his hind part." Patty closed her eyes and shook her head. "Where have you been all this time?"

"Las Vegas."

"City living. Why did you come back?"

Drew leaned against the wall and looked out at the parched landscape. "I spent my childhood wishing I was anyplace but here, living with Dwight. At first, I was relieved when I left Alabaster, but the longer I was away, the more I thought about home." He sighed and pressed his lips together. "Home should never be off limits. It's supposed to be the one place you can always come back to, a place where you're loved." Drew's voice cracked a bit.

"Sit down and rest your feet. I'm dying to know what you've been up to since you left."

"I worked at a hotel in Murray for a while, but it burned down so I moved on. I also worked in a club in Las Vegas for the last four years," he said dispassionately. The less glamorous he made his time away, the fewer questions she'd ask.

"That sounds drab. I thought you'd have a lot of flashy stories to share." She pouted and looked out yonder.

"It looks like everything went downhill after I left," Drew said. He looked out at the landscape filled with dead branches scattered below the trees and dry leaves stirring above the high grass.

"Not at first, but it did. Dwight was upset when you left. Although, I doubt it was out of concern. Without you, he couldn't get all the work done, so he lost business."

"I'm not surprised," Drew said with his eyes veering off to the empty tire-swing swinging beneath the cottonwood tree.

It didn't take much for him to envision a faded image of Arlene's pigtails floundering in the wind. Back then, he'd push her and she'd squeal on the way up, and giggle as she returned with her back against the wind.

"Is Arlene still around?"

"No, she's lived on the other side of town for quite some time, but her parents are still around. Her father used to come by to check up on Dwight. He'd ask about you from time-to-time which amounted to me shrugging my shoulders."

"I didn't expect her to stay around here. Are Daisy and Muffin still around?"

Wind swept through the valley, riling a thin layer of dust from the ground as Patty yawned and put her forearms on the hand rests.

"Daisy died four years ago. I don't know what became of Muffin. You'll have to ask Dwight."

He looked briefly at the planks of wood beneath his feet. Drew nodded with a sad look growing on his face. "I'm going for a walk. I'll be back."

He tightened his lips as he trekked down the steps, walked across the path to the hill, and descended on the other side. He sat near the edge of the pond, staring at the eerie image of himself and the trees that surrounded the body of water. Dead leaves sailed the surface and the surrounding area harbored a variety of prickly plants. His hearing sharpened as he heard something. He looked up with a gleam in his eyes that quickly faded when he realized that it was a frog coming up for air.

*16*

It didn't take long for Drew to acclimate to his surroundings, and naturally, he took on a good share of the responsibility for the upkeep of the land amongst other things. Thankfully, Patty was around to help with Dwight, but she had a tendency to be pushy at times.

She left the kitchen and walked over to Dwight in the living room. "Dwight, we need to talk." Patty looked at him closely as he sat close to the edge of the chair. Dwight nodded. "Drew, come here." He entered the room and stood beside her. "This is your son, Drew. He'll be taking care of you from now on. I taught him everything that Lucy showed me. Be nice to him." Patty narrowed her eyes and then turned to Drew. "If Dwight gives you any trouble, don't hesitate to call me."

Dwight's face stiffened. He eased back and slouched deeper into the chair.

"The refrigerator and pantry are stocked. Are you sure about this?" She asked.

"Yes, you've done more than enough. I'll handle it from here on out."

"All right then. Take care of yourself." She hugged him, went out the front door, and got into her car. Drew watched as her silver Pontiac left the yard.

Overall, things went as well as one could expect, but there were times when Dwight could barely get a word out, although, Dwight seemed more bothered by his inabilities than Drew was and it showed on his face. He had treated Drew like crap for most of his life and still, it was difficult to see a man who was once robust and independent now stagnant and dependent on the very person he had abused and pushed away.

He sat out front looking out at the expanse before him and then glanced at his father who was sitting in the rocking chair dressed in a plaid onesie. Dwight was calm today, but he had a bewildered look in his eyes and for some reason that made Drew uneasy. They sat on the porch for much of the day, listening to birds crooning in the trees, until Drew said something that came across more humorous than he'd thought and

Dwight chuckled for a while. This was how they spent many of their days.

When he wasn't caring for Dwight, Drew spent his free time cleaning the property. Within a few months, the ranch started to look alive again and Dwight's condition improved. He was even able to move around the house with little to no assistance.

❦ ❦ ❦

Before Drew knew it, he'd survived six months of dealing with Dwight. He went up the steps to the porch, sat down and drank water from a bottle he'd left on the porch earlier.

"Drew—" Dwight looked out from the porch at the manicured landscape that Drew had finished mowing minutes earlier.

"Yes, sir?" Drew looked at him as he swallowed.

"I'm sorry," he said in a low voice.

"For what?" A perplexed look spread on Drew's face.

"I remember…" Dwight clenched his eyes. A tear slipped from his right eye and rolled down his cheek. "You deserved better. I was awful to you. I hope that someday you can forgive me. My quarrel shouldn't have been with you. It should have been between Miranda and me." Dwight broke down and cried.

Drew backed into the seat behind him and sat there with a frozen expression that quickly morphed into an angry one. There was a part of him—albeit a small part—that wanted to say, 'Me—forgive you? No way! I'll forgive you when ducks do the River dance,' but what purpose would it serve? Drew exhaled instead.

All he could do was allow what Dwight said to churn in his mind for a spell. Tears began to fall one after the other and soon it felt as if they were competing to see who could shed the most. A time came when Drew had no tears left to shed, but Dwight kept going on as if he had an endless supply.

Drew sat there listening to crickets sing as the sky darkened. He sighed as he stood up, and went over to him. Drew closed his eyes as he patted Dwight's back.

"Let's not dwell on it, okay? I forgive you."

Dwight stopped sobbing and looked up at Drew. "Really?" He asked in a childlike voice.

"Yes. I forgive you." He stood beside him for a while and then returned to his seat on the other side.

Dwight watched the sun for the next fifteen minutes as it sank, creating an orange-yellow glow that capped the hills in the distance until it moved on to another hemisphere. Then, they went indoors.

Drew went to the kitchen, and Dwight straggled a bit before he entered the living room where he let out a deep sigh as he settled into the recliner and turned the TV on. Drew made a quick meal, and called Dwight to join him in the dining room.

"I have to get some supplies in the morning. Would you like to come?"

Dwight's face lit up and a wide grin spread on his face as he held the spoon above the bowl. "Yes, I want to go."

"Good. We'll leave right after breakfast."

Dwight nodded with a pasted grin that faded as he put a spoonful of corn chowder soup in his mouth.

❦ ❦ ❦

Early the next morning, the smell of sausage, eggs, and biscuits filled the air as they ate.

"I love sausage and eggs," Dwight said.

"I know; that's why I made it for you. Start eating. I want to leave within the hour, so we can be there by ten and back before noon."

After they were through eating, they left home and traveled to town. Dwight's forearm rested on the frame of the open window as he poked his head out, letting the wind palm his face. Within a matter of ten minutes, they were in town. Drew parked outside Rob's Hardware and stepped out.

Dwight stood on the sidewalk, waiting as Drew came around the car and they walked up the steps, side by side. Dwight began babbling spontaneously, catching Drew off guard, but his odd behavior didn't end there. He began to sway erratically and stumbled down the steps. Drew jogged down the stairs to catch him.

"Dad!" He held him as low squealing moans came from Dwight's lips and the left side of his mouth went off-center, misaligning sideways.

Rob, the owner of the store, heard the commotion and came out front. Drew looked up at him as he stood

127

in the doorway. "I need an ambulance," he shouted and looked at Dwight. "Dad!" Tears filled his eyes as he held Dwight close to his chest, rocking him gently.

## 17

An ambulance was there as quickly as one could expect in a rural area, and took Dwight to the hospital. Drew followed in his truck and spent the next three hours in the emergency room's waiting area. He was relieved when a doctor finally surfaced, but had to wait as he spoke to another family before coming to him.

"Are you Drew Tanner?"

"Yes. How's my dad?" He asked, moving closer to the slender man in a white lab coat holding a chart.

"Your father passed away shortly after he arrived," he said. "I'll take you to his room. It's down the hall."

Drew's heartbeat temporarily deafened him. He trailed the doctor in a dream-like trance state to a room in front of the nurse's station. He entered the room and saw Dwight lying on the bed with his eyes closed. Drew went up to him.

"I'm sorry for your loss. We did everything we could, but he had a massive stroke that triggered a heart attack."

He stood slanted at Dwight's bedside and held his hand as he thought about the countless times that he'd wished his father were dead. Now, all he wanted to do was to take it all back.

That day, not a tear was shed, but, as the days passed, tears flowed freely, leading up to the day of his funeral. A handful of people attended the service: Patty, Lucy, Dwight's former caregiver, and two distant cousins to name a few. Even Drew's roommates came down from Las Vegas the night before the funeral. There were others, but they were mostly people who'd done business with them over the years.

Patty approached Drew in the cemetery. She hugged him, and expressed her condolences.

"How are you holding up?" She asked.

Drew stared idly at the casket as it lowered into the ground. "I'm doing okay."

"Call me if you need anything." Patty's soothing voice echoed in his ear while she patted him on the back. "I mean it." Patty left his side and walked the thin path between the graves.

Drew stayed there until almost everyone left. Besides him, Derrick, Lou, and Scott remained. They left once the gravediggers began to shovel dirt in the opening, covering the casket, and took their time walking out to the car.

It was then Drew noticed a woman standing off in the distance amongst a collection of ornate headstones. He looked at her as she tucked portions of her dark hair behind her ear. When she looked his way, their eyes met. She was as beautiful as he remembered. They gazed at each other for a moment before she turned and walked away.

"Arlene, wait!" He shouted.

She stepped down from the sidewalk near where she was standing and walked to a car waiting at the curb. Arlene got in and drove away as Drew ran through the plots to the street. He stood there panting as he watched her car get smaller as it traveled farther away until it turned onto the main road.

Scott walked over and stood beside him. "Who was that?"

"An old friend."

## 18

Drew and his friends left the cemetery and drove to his place.

"You don't look too good. Are you okay?" Scott looked at him from the passenger seat.

Drew looked in the rear view mirror and shook his head when he saw Lou and Derrick were slipping in and out of sleep in the backseat like baby's taken for a ride.

"I'm okay under the circumstances," he said. Scott nodded and looked out at the expanse of unspoiled land.

A few miles down the road, Drew turned into his yard and parked. They got out, walked to the porch, and climbed the steps. Lou Chang sat on the railing. Derrick stood across from him with his back against the post and Drew and Scott sat on the chairs.

"Are you going to tell us who she is or am I going to have to pry it out of you? And don't give me that 'she's an old friend' line. It's not going to fly this time.

The look on your face when she drove away didn't give me that impression," Scott pried.

"We were best friends up until I left six years ago."

"If that's the case, why did she ignore you?" Derrick asked.

Drew glanced over at the cottonwood tree. "She's probably upset because I left town."

❦ ❦ ❦

The next day, Patty's silver Pontiac entered the yard and parked out front. Drew came out on the lawn to greet her.

"Hi." Patty smiled as their eyes met. "I came to see how you were doing."

"You could have called to find that out."

"I know, but people lie over the phone. I had to see for myself. That way I'll know if you're really okay." Patty hugged him. She saw three men coming out on the porch over his shoulder.

"Good afternoon," Derrick said. Scott and Lou echoed his sentiments and they introduced themselves.

"Hi, I'm Patty." She extended her hand and they shook it. "You guys look familiar."

"We were at the funeral," Lou said.

"That's right." Her eyes dilated.

"It's nice meeting you, but we're on our way out to do some work in the yard."

❦ ❦ ❦

Patty stuck around longer than usual, so Drew offered her a drink. She gladly accepted and he brought her a freshly squeezed glass of lemonade. Patty sat on the porch watching the fellows work as she sipped on the glass of lemonade and wiped her brow as if a heat wave was escalating and the ice was the only thing keeping it at bay. Her eyes trailed a meandering line of sweat running down the channel of Scott's back to his waistline saturating his jeans.

The fact that she was in her mid-forties didn't deter her hungry eyes from devouring every inch of his flesh and when she finished watching him, she moved on to Derrick, and watched him navigate the grass with the lawnmower.

"Patty," Drew said. She didn't reply, so he called out to her again. "Patty…" She looked at him. "What's Arlene address?"

Patty told him and gave him her empty glass. "Thank you. It was the best glass of lemonade I've had in a while." She licked her lips and stood up. "Well, I ought to be heading out. I have some errands to run in town. Call me if you need anything."

Patty went down the stairs fanning herself with her hands. She passed Lou on the way to her car, got in, and pulled away with a playful grin on her face.

## 19

The time Drew's friends spent in Alabaster went by faster than he imagined. The night before they were scheduled to leave, they reminisced about old times, shared new stories, and ended the night talking about Arlene. Drew blushed each time they mentioned her name.

It was as if he were back in grade school again, only this time he didn't have to deal with Peter, Wayland, or Brian. He was relieved when they finally dozed off. At least he wouldn't have to talk about her anymore.

The following day, they prepared for the ride back to Las Vegas.

"I wish we could stay longer, but you know Chip, he likes his hunk's to be on duty six days a week." Scott put his luggage out on the porch. "I still can't believe he gave us the time off to come out for the funeral. He must have really liked you," Scott said and smiled.

"I guess so."

"Take care." Lou Chang gave Drew a manly slap on the back as he side hugged him.

"I will."

"Make sure you get that girl," Lou Chang said.

Drew looked at him slightly annoyed as Lou took his bags to the red Mustang they'd rented. Derrick placed his hand on Drew's shoulder as he walked to the car with them.

"Talk to her, if that doesn't work, listen to what she has to say. A man that listens is appealing to a woman, at least that's what I've heard. Most of all, don't give up. If you do, it's a done deal."

Derrick removed his hand from Drew's shoulder and entered on the passenger side. By then, Lou Chang Wu was already lying in the back seat with the windows down and his feet hanging out the window.

Scott hugged Drew. "Stay in touch. Good luck with Arlene." Scott got in the car.

"Thanks. Have a safe drive," Drew said with a hint of sadness in his voice.

He watched as Scott drove out of the yard. Drew walked to the porch, ambled up the stairs, and sat on the top step, staring out at the meadow.

## 20

In the days that passed since the funeral, Drew couldn't get what happened at the cemetery out of his mind. Arlene's actions hurt more than he cared to admit, but for some reason, the day she threatened Dwight with a two-by-four came to mind. Drew smirked and shook his head. If he knew Arlene as well as he thought he did, she'd probably give him a black eye for leaving. Even with the dangers involved, he had to see her. He got in his truck and drove across town.

On the way there, he thought of what to say, but nothing seemed quite right. Before long, he entered her yard that was bordered by white fencing and parked in front of a small, mint-green house with yellow trim that sat on a mild slope amongst the ambience of a couple of red maple trees. As Drew stepped out, he noticed a persistent ding in the air. He walked to the house and strode up the brick steps. On the way up, he realized that the source was a peacock wind chime hanging from the yellow awning over the porch.

"Arlene." Drew called out to her as he stood there staring at the front door.

The door whined as it opened, Arlene came into view and stood in the doorway with a baby on her hip. She looked at him while the baby clasped a portion of her shirt.

"There's something I'd like to say—I didn't plan on leaving. I woke up that day, packed my bags, and went to see a man Dwight said was my father. Things didn't turn out quite like I'd hoped. I was torn after that as to what to do and ended up sitting on the roadside. That was when I was offered a way out, and I took it." She slammed the door in the midst of his explanation.

Her reaction upset him even more than her ignoring him at the burial. This time, it was up close and personal. There was no room to misinterpret her actions. Now, there was no doubt in his mind that she was upset with him.

Drew wanted to bang on the door until she opened it. He didn't care what happened after that as long as she acknowledged him. Instead, Drew stomped down the stairs to his car and left.

During the ride home, Arlene occupied his thoughts. Thinking back, he realized her stubborn streak had caused many debates during their childhood. Most of which ended with him accepting defeat, even when he was right. Deep down, he knew this disagreement would put all of the other disputes to shame.

He got home not long after he'd left her house, entered and went over to a small table where the phone was and made a call.

"Hey, Scott."

"Hi." Scott lay in bed, squeezing a stress ball. "It's nice hearing from you. How are you?"

"I've been okay." Drew took the cordless phone and sat in his father's recliner at the edge of the living room. "How are the guys?" Drew pressed the power button on the remote.

"They're okay. Derrick shared some interesting news the other day…"

"What news?" Drew didn't wait for him to finish.

"All this time, I thought that Derrick was reading muscle or naked magazines during his down time, come to find out that he was doing something far more productive. He was working on finishing his associate's degree."

"That's great news. Is he finished?"

"Two years ago."

"Really…I'm surprised that he didn't mention it," Drew said.

"Actually, I found out by accident. I went into his closet to retrieve something that he'd borrowed and that was when I noticed a stack of textbooks in the corner on the floor. So, I asked him about it. It turns out that, two years after Derrick started dancing he'd saved enough money to go back to school. He said he didn't want to disappoint me if he didn't follow through. So, he kept it to himself. I understand why he didn't mention it; he knows that I've always felt like I've disappointed him." Scott sighed.

"Cut yourself some slack. You're a good person. Anyone who says otherwise needs their head examined."

The volume on the TV increased on its own when a commercial came on, making it somewhat difficult for him to hear, so he cut the TV off.

"Thank you, I appreciate that. He's graduating with a bachelor's degree in two weeks. You're welcome to come." Scott's voice began to crack.

"I'll be there." Drew heard light sniffling on the other end of the line. "You must be proud of him."

"I am. I used to mull over the choices he made after his mom passed and often wondered what would've happened if I didn't become a dancer. He would probably be doing something else with his life."

"It was his choice. He chose to dance. Besides, he could have done worse," Drew said.

"That's true." Scott exhaled. The phone line went silent for a minute. "So… what's going on with you otherwise?" Scott threw the ball he'd been squeezing, and it bounced back at him.

"It took two weeks for me to finally go out to Arlene's place and she slammed the door in my face."

"Just take a step back and try not to take it personally. Arlene isn't any different from you. You've

143

been apart for six years. People change. Try not to lose any sleep over it." Scott sat up in bed. "Besides, if Arlene's that angry, that means she cares about you."

"I know. Back in the day, she beat the crap out of my dad for my sake and threatened to send her dad over to finish the job," Drew said and then began to laugh. "I miss her, Scott."

"I'm sure there's a part of Arlene that misses you too. All I can say at this point is, hang in there."

## 21

Once he recovered from the secondary blow, Drew went back to Arlene's place every day after he was through working for the next two weeks, but she never came to the door. At week's end, he decided to spare himself the humiliation and relaxed over the weekend instead, but on Monday he planned on going out to her place again.

He was about to get in his truck when a white-tinted truck pulled into the yard. Mr. Rexford, a former customer, stepped out and his showy white cowboy hat filled Drew's eye. He went over to greet him. Mr. Rexford tugged the waistline of his pants higher on his waist, but his enormous gut spilling over his belt made it difficult.

"I'd like to buy a load of hay."

Drew filled the order while Mr. Rexford sat on the porch enjoying the breeze. By the time he was through, the sun was lowering in the sky and what was left of it was shaded by thick gray clouds. Once Mr. Rexford's tailgate passed the gatepost, Drew left.

By then it was dark, but a pale streak of light remained in the distance. He drove the dark rural road to Arlene's house. His headlights lit the area as he entered her property, adding to the light that the small fixture above Arlene's front door gave off.

He stepped out of the car and jogged up the stairs. A shadow near the railing startled him and Drew almost lost his footing, but he held on to the rail.

"Arlene, is that you?"

She looked at him as she stood there in a thin, long nightshirt that clung to her body as a cool breeze swept through the porch.

He was taller and better looking than she remembered. "You're late! Six years late, to be exact." An angry rustic voice came from the barely lit porch and yet it brought him a fleeting joy.

Arlene moved closer to the door beneath the halo of the light that illuminated her dark hair, fusing with the obscurity surrounding them. Even in the dim light, her eyes were like daggers piercing him.

He cleared his throat. "I would have come earlier, but someone stopped by to purchase hay…" Drew stopped abruptly inflating his lungs with air. "I'm sorry for leaving the way I did. It was never my intention to leave town. It just happened."

"You could've let me know that you were leaving."

"I should have, but it wasn't possible at the time. I walked to Vernon Clevenger's house. Now, that's a six-mile walk from my home. But, it was all for nothing, he denied being my father. I left, walked three miles out until I couldn't go any further, sat at the side of the road and thought about everything that led up to that point. I couldn't take it anymore, Arlene. I just couldn't."

A baby's cry from within the home diverted her attention. "Excuse me." She left and emerged with a baby in her hand and closed the door. "This is my daughter, Emma."

Tight blonde curls draped close to Emma's round face as she gummed her index finger, rested her head on her mother's shoulder and stared at him.

He looked at her as she bounced Emma on her hip. "Why did you leave?"

147

"Dwight and I had one of the worst fights we've ever had the night before." Drew sighed. "If you'd seen what he did to me, you'd have given him a good beating. My face looked like I'd been kicked by a horse and other places on my body were purple."

Arlene clenched her teeth. "That no good bastard!"

"It's okay. I've gotten past it. I even forgave him before he passed. It did wonders for my spirit."

"I'm glad you've come to terms with it. Is there anything else you'd like to say?"

Drew stared at her idly for a while, not sure of what to say next. Unconsciously he said, *yes,* but in reality, he stayed mum. Arlene opened the front door, entered, and closed it behind her. Drew trudged down the stairs to his car and left.

During the ride home, he went over their conversation in his head and thumped the steering wheel. "Damn it! You know what? I've said what I had to say and if she can't understand that, then that's too bad."

*22*

Weeks later, Drew was on his way to Las Vegas, and in the matter of ten to twelve hours, he was walking on the strip's pavement, glancing up at billboard signs. The layout of the city was more than capable of putting New York's Time Square to shame with its colossal reproductions of the Statue of Liberty, Eiffel Tower, pyramids, and pharaohs—and they were all in the same city.

He could've taken a cab to the apartment, but he asked the driver to drop him off on the strip instead. Drew took in the attractions of the city as he walked to the apartment. On the way there, he saw an Elvis impersonator wearing the trademark studded white jumpsuit, singing "Hound Dog" as he twisted his hips. Drew stood there for a while watching him perform before moving on.

Oddly enough, he felt like he'd returned home. If it weren't for Derrick's graduation, Las Vegas would have seen the last of him, but it was a special occasion, so he planned to make the best of it.

His steps hastened as he neared the building. He entered the lobby of the apartment building, took the elevator up to Scott's floor, and knocked.

"Hey, welcome home," Lou Chang, said as he opened the door. They hugged as he entered.

"Where's everyone?" Drew's eyes traveled the room as he entered the living room and pulled the chain, opening the beige venetian blinds.

"Derrick is getting dressed. Scott stepped out but he'll be back shortly."

❦ ❦ ❦

Scott stood outside the front door and took a deep breath before he opened the door. He had been putting it off for some time now, but he couldn't any longer. Scott entered the apartment shortly after with a petite, dark haired woman on his arm. The petite woman in a black form-fitted dress with gold embellishments at the neckline and peep-toe platform heels stood beside him. He took her to the living room where Lou Chang and

Drew sat playing video games. He stood aside holding her hand.

At the same time, Derrick came down the hall dressed in a formal white shirt and black slacks, holding a wire hanger draped with his graduation gown.

"I'd like you guys to meet my girlfriend, Brielle."

"Congratulations on your accomplishment. I've heard so much about all of you. It's nice to finally meet you," she said.

*But we haven't heard about you.* "Thank you," Derrick said.

Brielle shook his hand and moved on to Lou and Drew, while Derrick eyed Scott.

"I'm ready if you are. The limo's waiting," Scott said. They left the apartment, and took the elevator to the lobby.

"We could have taken a cab," Derrick grumbled.

"I know, but it's a special occasion, so we're arriving in style." Derrick didn't counter Scott's argument once he heard that.

The ride to the venue was quiet with the exception of the elevator music streaming throughout the car. At least that was the case until Lou broke the silence.

"What are you going to do now that you've got your degree?" Lou asked.

Derrick gave him the 'buzz off' look and looked out the window. Lou helped himself to some champagne and turned to Drew.

"Would you like some?"

"No. Maybe later." Drew put his head back and closed his eyes.

"It will be flat later. Have some while it's still bubbly."

"Okay. Just a little—you know I'm not a drinker." After they'd had a couple of drinks, Lou and Drew mellowed out, but Derrick continued to hard nose Scott.

They arrived at the graduation's venue an hour later, passing a showy fountain spraying blue water ten feet into the air outside of the building. They entered the auditorium that was packed with family, faculty, and distinguished guests. The hour and forty-five minute ceremony included an inspirational speech by a guest speaker. Somehow, by the end of the speech, he inspired graduates and non-graduates as well.

Scott's eyes moistened when Derrick's name was called; Derrick went up on the stage for his rolled paper baton and Scott clapped anxiously and smiled until he returned to his seat. Seeing Derrick do what he had originally set out to do was a moment he'd longed for. His only regret was that their mother wasn't there to witness it.

❦ ❦ ❦

After the ceremony ended, they made their way through the crowd to the exit and waited for the limousine to arrive. They wait longer than expected. An hour later, the driver pulled into the pick-up area. He apologized as they got in and explained that he was stuck in traffic ten blocks away.

"We should go out and celebrate," Brielle suggested as the limousine pulled away from the curb.

"That's the best suggestion that I've heard all night," Lou said, followed by a hiccup.

Derrick looked at Lou. "What you need my friend is to go to bed."

"It's been a long day. We can do something another time. I'll have the driver take you guys home," Scott said.

Derrick's jaw tightened. He exhaled and tapped the handrail. The limousine parked in front of their apartment building twenty minutes later.

"It was nice meeting you all," Brielle said, brimming with excitement.

Derrick nodded and smiled. Whereas, Drew's head hung to the side as he slouched at the other end of the seat. Even so, he noticed the negative undertone of Derrick's actions.

"It was nice meeting you too," Drew said. Lou mumbled incoherently, but they got the gist of what he said.

"I'll see you guys in the morning," Scott said as they got out.

The trio entered the building and the limo drove away. Drew and Lou were beyond tipsy by then, so they went to bed, and Derrick pulled an all-nighter, watching old movies on Netflix.

❦ ❦ ❦

Scott entered the apartment a little after sunrise the following day, took care not to make too much noise in case they were still sleeping, and entered the kitchen. Derrick stood at the sink, rinsing out a cup.

"Good morning."

"Good? What's so good about it?" Derrick asked, looking over his shoulder.

"I hope this is not about—"

"I don't care who you date, but I don't appreciate the fact that you decided to bring a stranger who happens to be your girlfriend to my graduation without consulting with me first. That wasn't cool."

"I thought it was a good time to introduce her. After all, we've been dating for two years," he said.

Derrick's facial expression morphed from angry to confused. "If that's the case, why are we the last to know that you're in a relationship?"

"She's a celebrity, that's why! Brielle is actually Janae B. Scadden. The last thing she needs is TMZ's camera in her face when we're out on the town. Wait a minute! Do you know how hypocritical you sound right now? You haven't exactly been forthcoming either."

That lowered Derrick's peeved gauge a bit. "You have a point, but you should have chosen another day to introduce her to the circle."

"So, that was the singer/child actress, Janae Scadden?" Derrick asked.

"Yes."

Derrick nodded, grabbed a bottle of Coors from the fridge and left the kitchen. Drew narrowly missed bumping into Derrick as he was about to enter the kitchen, but backtracked. He'd always admired their brotherly bond, but it was hard to see them butting heads like this.

It was as if their respect for each other was unraveling before his eyes and there seemed to be no end in sight. It wasn't how Drew planned to spend his week here—tiptoeing around them—especially when their getting along was essential to the house running smoothly.

Meanwhile, Lou Chang Wu walked around the apartment as if everything was fine, but even a blind mouse could sense dissension among them. It wasn't that he didn't care, he just had other things on his mind, like improving his skills to be the best dancer in the club.

Later, Derrick walked through the hall in full workout gear and glared at Scott from the corner of his eye as they passed each other, taking care to keep his head straight. He left the apartment and went to the gym.

Lou shook his head; he had observed the brothers passing each other without acknowledgment. If only Derrick could let what Scott did slide, and move on, everyone in the house would be happy, but Scott's explanation for his gaffe only seemed to increase the tension between them.

## 23

Three days later, Scott invited Brielle over. They entered the apartment with bags in tow. Derrick visually scanned her without making it too obvious. She didn't look anything like the Janae Scadden he'd seen on TV, but if his brother said she was, he'd take his word.

Brielle tugged at her dark hair and the wig slid off her head with ease, revealing her wavy bronze hair. She ran her fingers through it.

"I've been dying to take that off ever since I left my place. It's *so* hot out there."

A stunned look crept onto Derrick's face, because now that she'd dropped the quasi emo look, she looked stunning in her floral mini sundress.

"I've invited Brielle over to have dinner with us," Scott said.

"Did you order out?" Lou asked.

"No, but she would like to cook dinner for us if that's okay with you guys?"

Everyone stayed quiet. She smiled.

"I'm making baked Shellfish marinated with seasoned butter, and onions drizzled with fresh lime juice. Homemade mashed potatoes with herbs is the side dish and I brought a bottle of wine too. After all, dinner wouldn't be complete without it." Lou Chang's face scrunched as she explained. Brielle noticed. "Don't worry. I know my way around the kitchen. If you like seafood, you won't be disappointed."

"This ought to be good." Lou Chang folded his arms as he smirked and relaxed on the sofa.

❦ ❦ ❦

An hour and a half after Brielle entered the kitchen, the air exuded a delectable mix of aromas that made their mouths salivate. She placed the prepared meal on the table and they sat down to eat. They ate small portions at first, which allowed the flavonoids to burst on their tongues.

Lou didn't expect this and by the look on Derrick's face, he didn't either. When Lou finally got around to looking Drew's way, his plate was already clean.

"This was delicious. Do you have enough for seconds?" Drew asked.

"There's plenty. I can prepare it for you." Brielle got up.

"That's not necessary. You've done enough. I can help myself." She sat down as Drew went to the kitchen.

"I'll have to agree with him. Your creation tastes better than some of the stuff I've bought in various restaurants around town," Derrick said.

"Oh wow, thank you." Brielle's eyes lit up.

"Yeah, what he said." Lou spoke with a mouth full of food.

Brielle smiled when she saw Drew return with his plate piled high.

"If you don't mind me asking, how did you two meet?" Drew asked as he sat down.

Scott looked at Brielle sitting beside him. "Should I, or will you?"

Her eyes brightened as she smiled. "I'll tell them. I was feeling crummy after my evening show, so my back-up singers, Colette and Leslie, convinced me to go out on the town with them. Somehow, she convinced me to go to Chip's Hunks. I concealed my identity by wearing the wig that I had on earlier. As soon as I entered the club, I saw Scott in the crowd. I smiled at him, but minutes later was mortified when he came out on stage. To make matters worse, Colette went on stage and slipped money in his pants. I still can't believe that she did that, but that is a whole other story. It was my first time going to a strip club, but I must admit that it was an interesting experience. You guys are good at what you do."

*Awkward* was the word that sprang up in Derrick and Lou's mind as they looked at each other.

"Anyway, so I left after the show. I didn't plan on returning, but I couldn't get him out of my mind. Three weeks later, I went back to the club and approached him after the show. I asked him to join me at a small restaurant nearby and he accepted."

Scott put his arm around her. "It wasn't the ideal way to meet someone, but we got past it."

Scott rubbed Brielle's shoulder briefly and removed his hand. He and Brielle finished eating.

Derrick smiled and nodded. "It isn't, but if you're happy that's all that matters." He got up and was about to carry his plate to the kitchen.

Scott and Brielle stacked their dishes and stood. "I'll take care of that," Scott said.

He put Derrick's plate with theirs and took them to the kitchen. Derrick went to the restroom. Now, Lou and Drew were the only ones left at the table.

Scott washed, while Brielle rinsed and put the dishes in the rack. Afterward, the two of them returned to the dining room and sat with the rest.

"Weren't you on TV?" Lou asked and scarfed down the rest of his food. Derrick returned to his seat at the table.

"Yes, I played the younger sister of Camryn, the love interest on *Zoe's Den*, a popular show featured on the Teen-n-mite Channel. The show was canceled after the fifth season, so I decided to pursue a singing career."

Lou and Drew finished their meal and they went to the living room. Derrick, Brielle, and Scott followed. She noticed a game case on the floor.

162

"Would anyone like to play against me in Mortal Kombat?" She asked.

"I'm always up for a challenge," Lou said. "I even have a black belt in this game."

"Lou, you have a black belt in *Bull Shitting*," Derrick said and laughed.

They took turns playing against each other while the chatter steadily rose in the room each time a fatality occurred. To her credit, Brielle beat just about everyone she played, except for Drew. All in all, they had a good time interacting until Brielle went home.

Naturally, things died down after she left. Lou and Drew left the room and moved on to do other things. Derrick and Scott remained and spoke candidly about the part they played in their dispute. At the end of their discussion, they apologized and hugged.

"I don't know about you, but I'm going to bed," Derrick said.

"I'm going to relax out here a little longer."

"Good night." Derrick left the room.

Scott nodded and a smile graced his face.

❧ ❧ ❧

Early the next day, Scott entered their rooms and roused them out of bed.

"Wake up. The sun is up and you should be too. Get dressed, there's someplace that I'd like to take you guys."

They got out of bed looking like tethered birds, but once they freshened up and ate breakfast they looked like polished gems. Later on, he and the others went down to the lobby expecting to catch a cab, but instead, Scott pressed the button on a keychain enabling a car alarm and walked to a silver Lexus. While they were sleeping, Scott picked up a rented convertible and parked it out front. They stood on the sidewalk looking at each other.

"What are you guys waiting for? Let's go."

They got in and he took them to Adventuredome Theme Park where they went on just about every ride. From there they went to Laser Quest, entered the dimly lit arena and walked through the foggy maze lit by strobe lights.

High-energy music streamed in the background as they moved stealthily, waiting for the opportunity to tag their opponent at a vulnerable spot. It was an intense game and they worked up a sweat while they were at it. After their quest ended, they followed the signs to the lobby and sat on the chairs out front.

"You sure know how to make up. We should fight more often," Derrick said laughing.

"Don't count on it. We've had a good time thus far, but I'm not done yet. Besides, I thought we should do something special before Drew leaves. Come on, we're going out for lunch."

Derrick nodded. Just when he thought they were on their way home, Scott sprang another surprise on them.

"But we're a mess," Lou said.

"Aren't you hungry?" Scott asked. "I know I am."

"I could eat a wagon wheel right about now," Drew said.

"I'm hungry too. Let's go," Derrick said.

They went to a Thai restaurant covered in paint splotches, ate until they were about to pop, and washed it down with wine. They engaged in lively conversation and cracked jokes about each other until Scott raised his glass.

"I'd like to make a toast to brotherhood, lasting friendships, and sweaty strippers. Cheers." Their glasses touched and Scott smiled as he looked at them.

## *24*

Days later, Derrick entered his boss' office.

"What brings you here?" He asked.

Derrick placed an envelope on his desk and slid it forward.

"What's this?" He opened the letter. "You're leaving us?" He put the letter aside and sighed. "I thought you'd change your mind and stick around after our chat the other day."

"I'm afraid not."

"I respect your decision. What do you plan on doing next?"

"I was offered a position as a talent management assistant with an entertainment company that recruits singers to headline shows in Las Vegas."

"That's a big deal. Congratulations. You've come a long way, but I have to tell you, I'm going to miss you, and the money you brought to the club." He shook Derrick's hand.

"I know, but I'll be putting my business management degree to good use. But before I do, I'm going to go out there and give the audience a show to put all of my other shows to shame." Chip smiled and then nodded as Derrick left his office and went to the dressing room.

Soon after, Derrick stood on the sidelines flexing his limbs like a boxer working the kinks out before a match, waiting for his cue.

"L-a-d-i-e-s!" DJ Tryst dragged the word. "Let's give a warm, final welcome to Nubian Python. He's heated up the stage for the past eight years, and tonight he's going to set it on fire." His charismatic oration riled the thick crowd from the booth.

Then, "Good Kisser" by Usher floated through the airwaves. A whistling intro spread through the room, and soon finger snapping joined the melody. In a matter of seconds, a heavy drumbeat vibrated from the speakers fused with a hypnotic bass sequence, and that's when Derrick moved toward the center of the stage, where slivers of light reflected off the parts of his well-oiled skin exposed from his knight gear.

The lights set off a glare from the iron headgear that also had a thin strip of metal protecting the bridge of his nose, and chainmail draped the back of his neck. He trailed his hand down the center of his grooved chest as the rapid flow of talk-singing followed.

Nubian's hips swiveled and popped outward as he switched his hips, while rotating his core in a circular motion. The fabric of the sleek, light-brown, knee-length *kirtle* that he wore, hung loose from his waist with an opening at each side that displayed his strong legs. With each seductive pivot of his hips, the center of his garment puffed out as if below the belt there was a gong struck with a beater. The crowd gasped and women in the front rows necks craned sideways.

If you listened close enough, you'd also hear fervent discussions. "Is that what I think it is?" One woman asked a woman sitting next to her.

But she wasn't the only one, others dared to lower their heads to see what lay beneath his skirt, only to come up with an astonished look on their faces.

His sultry dark amber skin tone oozed alpha in its most sensual form as he danced his way to the center of the stage, popping his pec's each time the drum beat sequence came around. Nubian flexed his bulky arms, spun around, and dropped to his knees, moving his shoulders as if he were doing the limbo and rested his back on the floor. His *beater* continued to animate his kirtle, thumping the thin cloth, imprinting the fabric as it recoiled from the stage floor.

In time, his back rose as he came up on his knees and stood up. That's when he saw a tall, dark beauty conservatively dressed in a fuschia dress with wedge heels. He went over to her and took her hand, urging her to come onto the stage with him as she shook her head, but eventually she gave into him.

Nubian Python kissed her hand, and brought her to the center of the stage. He spoke in her ear and in the blink of an eye, he picked her up and juggled her around his waist while her hair swathed her face. Her dress rode up as he maneuvered her in front of the crowd, exposing the lace undies covering her coco derriere.

The audience went nuts, and catcalls rose to a stellar pitch. Not to mention that the woman he'd enlisted for his act felt as though she'd swallowed her heart, and yet, she had a pasted grin on her face when he put her down. She stood there looking like she was about to fall, with a hand on her heart, blushing.

Nubian gave the crowd a view of his side and rotated his hips at her side, thrusting his center forward, allowing his membrane to swing at full throttle thumping her thigh as she clenched her eyes. She grinned awkwardly and scurried off stage while women in the audience squealed with excitement and fanned themselves.

DJ Tryst intervened near the end of the song. "Woo! Is it just me or is it hot in *here*?" He stomped his feet as he asked the question. "Ladies! Let's give it up for Nubian Python."

Deafening cheers filled the room as DJ Tryst clapped along with the audience. Derrick got all warm and fuzzy inside, bowed and walked off the stage. Scott stood on the sidelines waiting for his turn. He patted Derrick on the back as he was about to go down the hall.

"Good show."

Derrick nodded, "Thank you," and walked away.

Hours later, Chip locked the entrance to the club. Derrick walked with Chip to his car parked at the side of the building while Drew, Lou, and Scott waited at the curb for him.

"Are you sure you don't want to hang around a little longer?" Chip asked as he wobbled to the car.

"Yes. I'm sure."

"All right. As much as it pains me to see you go, give it your best shot. Show them that you're the man to beat. That's what made you successful in this business."

"Thanks Chip. Take care." Derrick shook his hand and jogged to where the others were waiting.

It was a slow, somber walk home. No one said much except to comment on something they'd seen on the way home, and once they got there, Derrick and Lou freshened up and turned in for the night. Drew and Scott stayed up for a while, watching a movie until Drew fell asleep on the couch with the remote slipping from his hand. Scott turned the TV off and went to bed.

❦ ❦ ❦

Drew woke the next day knowing that he had a long trip ahead of him. They all pitched-in to cook a buffet-style breakfast. After they'd finished cooking, they sat around the table and ate as much as they could handle.

"What time do you arrive in Alabaster?"

Drew looked at his watch. "It's hard to say. They often run late. It's a sixteen-hour trip. It could be shorter if they didn't make all of those stops."

"You'd be better off driving or taking the plane," Lou Chang said and shook his head.

"That's easy for you to say, but when you have to shell out six-hundred plus dollars for the ticket you'll be singing another tune."

"Your right—a broke tune." Lou Chang huffed.

"Besides, my truck's been acting up lately."

They chatted for a while before he brought his luggage to the front door.

"Have a safe trip," They said.

Drew left, took the elevator to the ground floor, and caught a cab. He gazed out the window as the cab pulled away from the building and traveled down the road. It wasn't that long ago he'd gotten off the bus, and now he was on his way back to Alabaster, even though the only thing waiting for him back home was an empty house filled with bad memories and a yard filled with work.

## 25

Eventually, the Las Vegas strip blurred as they traveled farther from its center. A half-hour later, the cab dropped Drew off at the bus station. He boarded the bus, and shortly after they were on the highway eating miles by the gallon.

Drew dozed off when it was quiet but was awakened by his neck snapping back to hear a louder than life cell phone conversation, and when they made a rest stop at a layover there was always someone who felt the need to buy seafood or a sandwich with extra onions that would essentially make the entire bus funky. But it didn't end there. During the longest stretch in between rest stops, the bathroom's itinerary crept to the interior of the bus, tickling the nose of innocent bystanders.

Drew was thankful when the bus neared his stop, and parked outside the terminal door. He stepped down from the bus and walked a block to the turnoff of the long stretch of road that led to Alabaster, Nevada. The thought of having to hitch a ride the rest of the way only added to his fatigue.

Drew waited at the side of the road until his feet hurt, and then he sat on his duffel bag. After eighteen hours, if you included the time he was waiting at the roadside, he was dog-tired. He scooted down on the grass, leaned back against the duffel bag, put his grandfather's hat over his face and fell asleep.

A blaring horn cut through the sounds of nature, rousing him from sleep. Drew lifted the hat from his face and sat up.

"I thought you were dead or sleeping. I'm glad it was the latter. I'm off the clock right now, and I'd like to stay that way."

Her elbow rested on the frame of the open driver side window as she sat in an older model Ford Ranger. A gust of wind tossed thick ringlets of her blonde hair from her shoulder.

"What are you doing out here? There's nothing out here for miles, besides the bus and a gas station."

"I'm waiting for a ride."

"Are you waiting for someone in particular?"

"Not really. I'm trying to hitch a ride."

"You're failing miserably. You have to be awake for that to work, and showing some leg wouldn't hurt," she said and laughed. "Hitchhiking is a dangerous venture."

"I know, but I'm good at reading people." Drew assured and chucked the hat on his head.

"Right…" she said pursing her lips and then nodded. "That's what my last victim said."

"Huh?" A perplexed look spread on his face.

She smiled. "I'm just testing your people reading skills. There's no need to be alarmed. I'm a dispatcher at the police headquarters five miles from here."

Drew exhaled and smirked. "How far are you going?" She asked.

Her deep-set, pale blue eyes looked him over as he responded, "Alabaster."

"You're in luck. I can take you five miles shy of that part of town, but you're on your own after that. I'm Tammy by the way." She extended her hand.

"Drew. It's nice to meet you," he said and shook her hand.

"Are you coming or not? I'd like to be home before dark."

Drew got in and Tammy drove toward town, leaving a stream of exhaust smoke behind her. Tammy's foot lay heavily on the gas pedal, taking him closer to his destination in no time. She'd reached the point where she would be dropping him off, stopped the car and Drew stepped out. He thanked her and waved as she drove away.

Now that he was five miles from Alabaster, tired couldn't begin to describe how he felt, but he didn't feel like waiting for a passerby to take him the rest of the way. Drew started walking toward the downtown area, feeling like a man straggling through the desert to a water hole. He trod the rest of the way on sheer determination alone, and stopped the moment he saw the outline of the town as it became more clear. Drew rested his hands on his knees and took deep breaths. *Just a little bit further,* he told himself, *your almost there.*

*Part Four*

# The Remnants

# 26

The convenience store was his first stop. He was about to enter when he saw Mrs. McQuillen stepping out of the apothecary next door. Her broad straw hat came into view while the wind flirted with her white, lace-trimmed dress, making it cling to the love handles at her waist and disturbed ringlets of her strawberry blonde hair.

She saw Drew out of the corner of her eye and went over to him. "I'm sorry that I wasn't able to make it to your father's funeral. I had the *MRSA* virus at the time, the one that everyone was trying to avoid." She sighed. "Thank God, I survived it." She rested her hand on her hip. "I am glad Arlene was able to go. I thought she'd be too busy dealing with her own loss." She exhaled deflating her cheeks. "She proved me wrong."

"What loss?" Drew asked.

Mrs. McQuillen fanned herself with a sales flyer from Rob's Hardware store and looked absently off in the distance.

"It's no secret that Arlene wasn't a fan of your father, but she wanted to be there for your sake." Mrs. McQuillen eased closer to him. "You should know that she cried herself to sleep for quite some time after you'd left. All she had to do was get in a room by herself and she'd cry until her eyes were swollen. We tried our best to console her, but Arlene pushed us away. I don't think she ever got over it either, but don't tell her I told you so." Mrs. McQuillen let out a deep breath. "It was nice seeing you, but I should get going. Brett's waiting for me over at the market. Take care." She walked away fanning herself.

For some reason, he thought of the conversation he had with Scott days earlier as they relaxed in the living room and his forehead rippled.

*"How is it going with Arlene?"* Scott had inquired.

*"I tried to explain to her why I left. She listened and then she left me hanging there,"* Drew answered.

*"At least you tried. Maybe it's time to let her go."* It wouldn't be easy, but he was willing to let her go, at least until now, after the conversation he had with Mrs. McQuillen.

❦ ❦ ❦

He was dirt-tired by the time he got home, but instead of resting, Drew got into the truck and turned the key. It didn't start, so he tried again, and this time it did. He drove to Arlene's place. As he entered her yard, he saw her sitting on the steps.

He parked, got out of the truck and walked to her. As he neared, Drew realized that Arlene was sobbing. Emma was crying in the background too, and it sounded as if she'd been bawling for quite some time.

"Is everything okay Arlene?"

She continued to weep. Drew took her by the hand, urging her to stand and led her to the front door. They entered and he stood at the edge of the living room beside her. Drew left Arlene and followed Emma's cries down the shadowy hall lined with photos of Arlene from her childhood. He smiled as he caught a glimpse of a picture of her with frayed pigtails and a missing front tooth.

Drew continued down the hall to a room in the back where Emma's heaving cries filled the room, old tears smeared her cheeks, and fresh ones washed away the salty residue. Emma flailed her legs, tensing them outward with each pitch-filled wail, and the center of her pampers hung down to her knees.

He stuck his head out in the hall. "I think she needs to be changed."

Arlene didn't respond. She just stood there. Drew sighed as he turned his gaze back to the child's bedroom. He scanned the room for anything pertinent to the task and saw a stack of pampers and a container with wipes. Near it was a changing table at the far right of the room.

He picked her up and laid her on the table. His nose scrunched as he opened her soiled diaper. The ammonia-like scent of urine wasn't the most pleasant odor whether it came from the very young or old. He changed her diaper but put her Pampers on backwards. Drew picked her up and took her to Arlene.

"I don't know what's going on with you, but Emma's depending on you." Emma reached for Arlene and she took her. She put her head on her mother's shoulder and looked at Drew. "Are you going to tell me what's wrong or not?"

"I don't want to talk about it. You should go. You're used to walking away. I've come to expect that from you, and Drew, you don't have to look back this time."

"I didn't leave because I wanted to. I left because I didn't know what else to do. I thought you'd understand that," Drew said in a country accent that had thinned over the years.

This time he didn't plan on waiting around for her to shut the door in his face. Drew went out the door, and it slammed behind him. He walked to his truck and drove in a hurry out of her yard, leaving a trail of dust behind him.

❦ ❦ ❦

Later that evening, while he lay in bed, Arlene's words taunted him. *'You're used to walking away. I've come to expect that from you, and Drew, you don't have to look back this time.'*

Tears slipped from his eyes, leaving droplets on the pillowcase beneath his head as he looked up at the ceiling. He was used to rejection; in fact, he'd dealt with it most of his life, but he had someone that was there for him during the best and worst of times. Now, Arlene McQuillen didn't want to have anything to do with him, and it hurt more than words could say—so much so that he cried himself to sleep.

*27*

He woke the next day with more determination than he had the day before. Things hadn't gone quite the way he hoped, but he wasn't going to give up on her. Drew got dressed, and drove back to Arlene's place. He didn't even bother to eat. It was the furthest thing from his mind.

Normally, he'd start with the customary morning salutations, but there wasn't anything *good* about his morning thus far. She came out as he parked in her yard and sat in a chair on the porch. Drew went up the steps, stood in front of her and wasted no time giving her a piece of his mind.

"I've tried talking to you, but you keep shutting me out. At this point, I don't know how much longer I can keep this up." He huffed. "If I can forgive Dwight, who treated me worse than he did our dog, *you* can forgive *me*. You know what? You don't have to forgive me, but I'd like for us to go back to being friends." He sighed and looked down at his feet.

She looked at him and then out at the field, filled with dandelions and butterflies chased by the brisk wind.

"I used to wonder what your life was like after I left," Drew said.

Arlene swallowed and tightened her lips. "Isn't it obvious? I got married." She splayed her left hand displaying the wedding band on her ring finger.

When he heard she was married, his eyes twitched. "Who'd you marry?"

"You know him, Brian's my husband."

"Wait a minute, Brian Fowler, the kid who ran through the playground peeling his shirt off as a gang of bees stung him in grade school after we dared him to climb a tree?"

Arlene giggled, "Yes—that Brian," she said and laughed harder than before, but tears soon followed. "I'd forgotten about that." She wiped her eyes.

"Where is he?"

"He enlisted in the army. After his basic training, they sent him to Afghanistan." As she continued, her lips began to tremble. "Three months later, a roadside bomb went off when his unit neared a checkpoint. The explosion tore the Humvee apart, and a large piece of shrapnel punctured Brian's lung and another severed his carotid artery. He died on impact. It's been a year since his death." Arlene clenched her teeth as she tried not to cry. Her voice hoarsened. "At the time of his death, I learned that I was four weeks pregnant with Emma." She sat there, staring at nothing in particular.

"I'm sorry for your loss." The pit of his stomach twisted as he spoke. She had more on her mind than he'd imagined.

Arlene nodded. "Emma won't know what her dad was like." The urge to cry intensified, but this time, she let her tears flow freely.

Drew moved closer and rubbed her back. "Tell Emma about him. He'll live on in the memories you share and in the hearts of his loved ones as long as you let him."

"I'll try to keep that in mind," she said and sniffled. "The only other time I've felt this kind of loss is when you left. A part of me wilted, and all I could do was cry. I don't want to go through that again."

The sounds of nature took over for a while, and then Arlene looked at him with visible pain in her eyes. "You've been gone a long time, but to me it seems like the other day that I went over to the pond and waited for you. But you never came, so I went to your house and asked Dwight for you. At first, he said you weren't there. I told him that I would come back later. That's when he said, 'Don't bother. Drew's gone and I don't think he'll be back.' He said it like it wasn't a big deal. If I had known what he did to you, I would have kicked him in the shin."

Drew smirked. "Yeah, I'm sure you would've. I'm sorry—"

"I'll be the first to admit that I've been too hard on you, but… it's just that… I said '*I love you. You matter to me*,' I thought it meant something to you, at least enough for you to stick around, but I understand why you left. I just wished you'd kept in touch." Drew held her hand and sighed with a heavy heart, but he was relieved to hear her say that.

He left Arlene's place feeling hopeful that they would get past their misunderstanding and go back to being friends.

## 28

From then on, the upkeep of the land kept Drew busy, especially now that hay was bountiful, but there was more to life than working day in and day out. He walked to the porch to escape the oppressive heat that had gripped the area for the past two days. Sweat ran down his face and neckline to his chest forming a thick line of sweat that saturated the middle of his T-shirt.

Drew grabbed a face towel he'd left on the railing as he entered the house, wiping his face and neck. He sat on a wood chair next to a small accent table in the living room, lifted the phone from its cradle and phoned Scott. He could always count on him to brighten his mood and it was a plus that he was also a voice of reason.

"Hi, Scott." Drew smiled at the sound of his voice.

"I was just about to call you."

"How are things over there?" Drew asked.

"It's been good. Derrick moved out. It's just Lou and me now. Unfortunately, I don't think that I can ever get rid of him, even if I tried. It's cool though. He keeps things interesting around here. I have to give it to him, when Lou says he's going to do something, he does it. He's the top dancer in the club now, and the customers are loving every minute of it."

"That's good to hear. I know he's wanted that for some time now. How's your lady friend?"

"She's fine. In fact, that's why I was going to call you. I asked her the most important question a man can ask a woman, and she said yes. We're getting married."

"Congratulations. When's the wedding?"

"Sometime later this year. We haven't scheduled a date yet. I'm just thankful that we found each other."

"I'm happy for you. I have some good news of my own. Arlene finally stopped giving me the cold shoulder."

"Wait a minute. I thought you said you were—I have to give it to you—you're persistent." Scott snickered. "So, everything is good in *friend* land?"

"Yeah, it looks that way," Drew said and sighed.

"You don't sound too happy about that."

"I am, it's just that—oh, I don't know."

"It sounds to me like the friend zone isn't as cool as you thought it would be. Sometimes, the mind and heart choose a different path, but if all else fails, you can always follow her around."

Drew chuckled. "Well, when you put it that way, who wouldn't?"

"I have more exciting news to share," Scott said and Drew braced himself.

"I am no longer working at the club." He gave Chip his resignation letter, putting his exotic dancing career behind him. "I've been working on something for a while and it should be ready in a month or so."

Scott couldn't wait to share the news now that he had gotten his priorities straight and his plans were on the verge of coming to fruition after spending the past few months doing the legwork.

He glanced at his watch. "I'll tell you more about it later. I have an appointment. We'll talk again soon," Scott said.

"Take care, bye." Drew put the phone down and he eased back in the chair.

## 29

Autumn approached, bringing with it cooler temperatures. The downside was that there was less to do around the yard, besides the occasional raking of leaves and removal of dead branches strewn below the trees. It gave him more time for himself, but Drew spent most of it cleaning the house. He packed up all of Dwight's clothes and put them in a box with the intention of donating them. When he was done, he stood near the closet in Dwight's room, looked over at the nightstand and walked over.

He opened the top drawer that was filled with papers and on top was an envelope. He picked it up, taking note of the sender. His forehead rippled as he tapped it against his open hand. He put it on the nightstand, left the room, and closed the front door on the way out.

Drew got into his truck and drove to the hardware store in town to pick up a roll of trimmer line for the Weed Wacker. As Drew stepped out of his car and walked to the store's entrance, he heard someone call out to him. He turned in the direction he heard the voice coming from, but he didn't see anyone that looked familiar, so he continued walking. Then, he heard his name again.

"Yes. Who is calling me?"

Drew came face-to-face with a bearded man that reeked of whisky and urine. His hand instinctively covered his nose.

"It's me, Wayland." The slender man with matted black hair and a thick locked beard came closer to him.

"Wayland? Peter's brother from grade school?" Drew lowered his hand.

"Yes," he said and laughed in a manner that sounded like he was imitating the beat box.

Wayland smiled, displaying teeth that looked like they'd been through hard times, stained to a murky brown and covered in plaque. Drew tried not to look alarmed by Wayland's appearance, but it troubled him.

"Do you have a couple of dollars you can spare?" Wayland asked as he placed his hand on Drew's shoulder. Drew opened his wallet and gave him ten dollars.

"Thanks. It's good to see you," he said.

"You're welcome. What are you doing with yourself?"

"I'm just around, you know, doing stuff. You know how I am."

Drew exhaled. He'd heard rumors, but now he was seeing firsthand how much Peter's death affected him. Drew said something to Wayland before he entered the hardware store, but as he exited the store, he noticed that Wayland was exactly where he left him, and by the looks of it, he was in another world and hadn't heard him. Drew got in his truck and drove away.

❧ ❧ ❧

Once Drew left, Wayland snapped out of his daze and went to the liquor store across the street. Minutes later he emerged with a paper bag in hand, scrunched to the shape of the bottle inside. Wayland twisted the cap off as he walked to a small park nearby and drank an ounce. He sat on the bench, and set the bottle down beside him. Tears slowly filled his eyes as he sat there thinking about what Drew said with the taste of the beer souring in his mouth.

Wayland picked up the forty-ounce bottle and drank as he clenched his eyes. For some reason, he couldn't bring himself to drink another drop, no matter how much he wanted to.

"Damn you, Drew Tanner," he yelled.

Wayland threw the bottle on the floor and it shattered, releasing foamy liquid on the asphalt below. He held his head, crouched low and bawled as an unbearable pressure built in his head—to the point that it felt like his head was going to explode. Wayland stood, but kept a hand on his forehead as he left the park.

❦ ❦ ❦

Meanwhile, on the way to Arlene's place Drew couldn't help but think about his run-in with Wayland and how awkward he felt. Arlene came out on the porch as she saw the truck entering her property. He got out and walked to the steps.

"You're making it a habit of coming around here. Don't you have anything better to do?" She asked with

197

Emma on her hip. Arlene put Emma down and she crept in Drew's direction as he came up the steps.

"Yes, but I'd rather be here instead of being in that empty house by myself."

Emma's bent knees trembled as she balanced her center, straightening her body as she rose vertically and then she put one foot forward and then the other, just as Drew looked down. Emma stretched out her hands, smiling as she walked toward him and gurgling when he smiled at her. He lowered his body and reached for her. Emma held Drew's arm as he picked her up.

"Did you see that?" Drew asked with a chuckle.

Arlene's smile eclipsed the sun. "Yes, I've been waiting fourteen months to see that," she said with a wide gaze. "Those were her first steps."

"I thought babies usually walk by their first birthday."

"That's usually the case, but not always. I had a rough pregnancy."

Arlene's eyes grew teary. She reached to hug the two of them just as Drew turned his head to accommodate her, but instead their foreheads bumped and recoiled, causing their lips to touch.

"I'm sorry. I didn't mean for that to happen," he said.

While he apologized, he reminisced about the day she kissed him on the cheek when they were teenagers, but this time it was on the lips, and his cheeks reddened. Looking at Arlene, he noticed that her cheeks were red too.

"It's okay," she said. She looked at Emma. "Mommy's so proud of you!"

Emma opened her arms to her and Arlene took her. She set Emma down to stand in front of her and eased away with her arms splayed. Emma's legs trembled as she walked to her. She held on to her mother's open arms and Arlene picked her up, threw Emma in the air above her head, and caught her as gravity pulled Emma back to her.

She hugged Emma as she giggled. "I'm so proud of you."

Meanwhile, Drew tried to calm his racing heart as he looked at them.

"What are you guys up to today?" He leaned against the post framing the awning of the porch.

"Nothing much. I planned to go to town and pick up some groceries. Would you like to come with us?" She asked.

"Sure, I don't mind tagging along," Drew said without giving it a second thought. "You'll never guess who I saw in town not long ago."

Arlene propped Emma on her hip and trekked down the steps to her car. "Just tell me, I hate guessing."

"Wayland."

Drew got in the passenger seat of Arlene's blue soft-top jeep and he told her all about his encounter with Wayland. She strapped Emma in the car seat, got in and drove out of the yard.

"So, what did you say to him?" She asked.

"'I dare you to do better than what you're doing now.' Wayland stood there like someone had yanked his chain too hard, and from then on, he was no longer audible."

"Let's hope that your words reached him. You guys used to live for dares."

"True," he said and chuckled lightly.

Drew sat there, stealing glances at her as the wind swept through her hair, eyeing her smooth, seemingly candied skin.

## 30

"I've always wondered what your life was like after you left here," she looked at him for a split second before her attention returned to the road ahead.

He nodded. "It wasn't as exciting as you'd think. I hitched a ride to Trepidation, and then got a ride to Murray. I worked at The Back Leg Inn for two years until some Meth-head burned it down."

"Murray—that one horse town?" She questioned, but she didn't expect a reply.

Arlene entered the market's parking lot, and parked near the store's entrance. They entered the market and she pushed the cart through the aisle, adding items as she went along while Emma tapped the handle of the cart seat.

"What did you do after the motel burned down?"

An older couple passed them in the aisle as Drew slid his hands in his pant pockets.

"I went to Las Vegas." He looked at his reflection on the polished tiled floor.

"Now, that sounds like fun."

"I guess. It depends on how you look at it—"

"Hand me a can of red beans, please?" Arlene pointed at the shelf to the right of him and Drew put the can in the cart.

"I think that's it. Let's go," she said.

Arlene pushed the cart to the register and put her items on the conveyor belt. A series of obnoxious beeps followed as the cashier scanned her items.

"Fifty-seven dollars, thirty-two cents is your total," the cashier said.

Arlene pulled her wallet from her purse.

"I'll get it," Drew said before Arlene could take her money out.

He paid and they walked to the Jeep and within five minutes, they were on their way back to her house. They didn't have that far to go, and were approaching the stretch of road that led to her home.

"Would you like to stay for dinner?" She asked as she parked outside her home.

"Sure. It beats eating alone, that's for sure," Drew said.

She took Emma from the child car seat and Drew removed the groceries. They entered the home, and she put Emma in the playpen in the living room, while Drew put the groceries on the kitchen counter. Arlene joined him in the kitchen.

"What was it like in Las Vegas?" She wiped her hands on the kitchen towel.

"There were lots of things to keep the average person entertained, but it was tough to make ends meet. I had a job, but that didn't last too long. I barely made enough to pay for a room."

Arlene listened while she seasoned the slab of steak she'd laid on a baking pan, drizzled with olive oil. He observed as she cut an onion, unhinged the rings, and arranged them on the steak. She glanced across the hall and saw Emma sleeping in an awkward position in her playpen.

"Drew, can you straighten Emma out for me, please?" She said and chuckled. "She falls asleep in the weirdest positions at times. My favorite is when she props her butt up."

Drew smiled. "Sure." He walked across the hall and laid Emma flat on her stomach.

Later on when she'd finished cooking, they sat opposite each other at the table. "I'd love to hear more about your time away," she said, resting her chin on her raised hand.

Drew sliced into a portion of his steak. "Do you want to know everything?" He asked and then put a fork full of meat in his mouth.

"Everything," she said with an inquisitive spark in her eyes.

"Well…" He put the fork down. "I also worked at a small restaurant, but that job didn't last long. After that, I was out of luck—adrift.

"And?"

"I was virtually invisible to people as they walked by when I lived on the streets. It didn't take long for me to realize that I couldn't eat my pride, so I swallowed it and begged for change."

The light in Arlene's eyes dimmed as her eyes moistened. "I had no idea you had such a hard time."

Arlene continued to eat, but she paused and looked Drew's way, observing him as he ate the remnants of food from his plate. She couldn't help but feel awful about the way she'd treated him.

"Dinner was delicious. I can see that your mother's cooking skills rubbed off on you."

Arlene smiled. "Thank you."

She slid her plate to the side, eased out of her chair and stood at the end of the table. Arlene walked to him and reached for his plate.

"I feel terrible about the way I treated you."

"Don't be… you had every right to be mad at me. I should have written or called to let you know that I was okay."

Arlene took the dishes to the kitchen, turned on the faucet, flung the kitchen towel over her shoulder, and stared at the running water for a while. She snapped out of her daze, washed the dishes, and put them away. Drew entered the kitchen and stood beside her.

"Don't beat yourself up about it. I survived the ordeal. Actually, I'm a better person having gone through that experience."

She turned and looked at him. "How did you make it?" Arlene asked as they left the kitchen and made their way to the living room.

Drew sat next to her on the sofa. "I didn't think I could last a day on the streets until I ran out of options. At first, I tried staying at a homeless shelter. It was the logical thing to do, after all, I didn't have any family there, but it was an unnerving experience. Not even my shoes were safe. My breaking point was when I woke one night to see a man holding a rusty knife to my throat. After that, I went twenty-eight hours without sleeping. It was crazy. So, I decided that I couldn't stay there anymore." Arlene wove her fingers through his and held his hand. "It got so bad that I had to ask strangers for help. One night, I was begging for change when a man came my way as I crouched on the sidewalk. He paused long enough to give me a roll of bills and continued down the path." Drew smiled. "I can tell you, that because of his offering I was able to eat a decent meal for a week and a half. Weeks later, the same man extended a helping hand that changed my life. I don't even think he knows it. Considering that, the time I spent in Las Vegas wasn't all bad."

Arlene cozied up to him. "Tell me about him."

Drew put his arm around her shoulder, like he used to when they were teenagers. "I didn't know anything about him at first, but he seemed genuine when he offered to help. Afterward, I found out that he was an exotic dancer."

Arlene tapped his knee. "You're kidding, right?"

"No, he was a stripper. In fact, I was sleeping on a pile of boxes in the alley behind his workplace and that's when he offered me a place to stay."

"He sounds like a brave, selfless man."

"He is. He even got me a job at the club."

Her eyes widened. "As a stripper?"

Drew thought for a second and smirked. "Yes, I became a stripper. I can dance for you if you want me to."

He got up, and swayed his hips to his own melody as Arlene clenched her eyes and blushed. Drew held her hand and pulled her up to him while she giggled nervously.

"Stop goofing around," she said, embarrassed by the naughty places her mind ventured to, *she* envisioned Drew, bare-chested in chaps, dancing under the stage lights.

He raised her chin with his finger. "I'm just kidding." His lips widened as he smiled. "I was a sweeper, collecting the tips that the audience tossed the dancers' way."

Arlene's heartbeat leveled off as the scandalous visions faded, but her thoughts raced onward.

"No matter how bad things got, thinking of you always made everything better. You were the constant—the only consistent happy memory that I could hold on to—to give me hope."

They lessened the space between them, hips touching as their lips locked. It was the first time they'd been close enough to feel each other's breath. When Drew wrapped his arms around her waist, everything that she was thinking about seeped from her mind.

Arlene wrapped her arms around his neck. Her lips pressed against his in a steady intoxicating kiss, traversing in a sensual manner, and soon their tongues were enmeshed. The room grew hot in an instant, too hot for clothes, and soon the urge to peel them off intensified. She checked on Emma out of the corner of her eye. Thankfully, she was still sleeping. Drew released her lips.

"We shouldn't, Emma's here," she said blushing.

Drew put his lips to her ear, before she could say anything else. "We can take this to the bedroom."

Arlene melted in his arms as he swept her up off her feet and carried her to the bedroom. He placed her on the bed, lay atop her and went in for another kiss. At that moment, the beginnings of a moaning cry came from the living room. He raised his body, eased off her and lay on the bed face up.

Arlene sighed and sat up in bed. "I'll go check on Emma."

She left the room, and Drew lay there with a dreamy look on his face. Deep down, he knew that their friendship was forever changed. There was no turning back after the kiss they'd shared, and yet he was uncertain where their relationship would go from there, but he knew that he no longer wanted to be just friends, and based on her reaction to his kiss, neither did she.

Arlene returned with Emma on her hip. "You sure know how to crash a party," Drew said and then smiled and Emma giggled as if she understood what he meant. "It's late. I should go home."

Arlene pouted. "We can finish what we started another day."

Drew smirked, "I know." He smiled as he walked to her and kissed her on the cheek. "I'll call you in the morning." Emma touched his cheek with her open hand. He held her hand and kissed it. "Bye."

## 31

Patty's Pontiac entered the yard early the next morning. She got out and walked to the porch. Not long after, the floorboards creaked as she came up the steps and knocked on the front door.

Drew peered through the window near the door and sighed. Somehow, he got the feeling that she didn't subscribe to the notion of calling before dropping by unannounced, but he knew better than to make a fuss about it. He opened the door.

"Good morning." She entered the home. "What've you been up to?"

She went into the living room, grabbed the remote from the coffee table, sat in Dwight's recliner and put the TV on.

"I've been cleaning Dwight's room and donated his clothes to the mission."

"That was nice of you." She folded her legs. "If it were me, I'd put his clothes in a pile out in the field, set them on fire, and do a rain dance while I'm at it," Patty spewed.

He laughed under his breath. "Would you like something to drink?"

"A glass of water, please." She answered, focusing on the TV screen.

Drew went to the kitchen.

"When will your friends be back?" She elevated her voice.

"I don't know if they'll be back, but I wouldn't rule it out. What's it to you?" He gave her the glass of water and she placed it on the coaster on the small table beside her.

"They're easy on the eye, that's why."

"The women at the club would agree with you. They're exotic dancers."

Patty moistened her lips. "I'm no spring chicken, but if Susan Sarandon can reel in a young stud, so can I."

Drew laughed. "I'll take your word for it. Seeing that you're here, there's something that I'd like to show you. I'll be right back."

Drew left the living room and traveled down the hall to Dwight's room. He picked up the letter he'd left on the nightstand weeks earlier and gave it to her. She looked at the sender's address: DNA Diagnostics.

"I've seen this before. What do you want to know?"

"Did he say anything to you about it?"

"I asked him about it when I first started looking after him, but I couldn't get him to focus long enough to give me a straight answer. I even asked Lucy, but she had no clue either."

Patty gave him the letter. Drew opened it and read it line-by-line. His face grew pale and clammy. The note slipped from his hand and swayed to the floor. He slumped down into the sofa behind him.

"What's wrong?" She eased to the edge of the recliner.

A tear ran down his cheek. "All those years that he mistreated me because he thought I wasn't his son, when in fact he was my father all along."

Patty picked up the letter and read it. "Well I'd be dammed. Did you notice the date on this?"

"Yes. It was processed a month after I left. You'd think that they would have taken a paternity test when I was a baby."

"That would've been the sensible thing to do. I wasn't a fan of Dwight, but to be fair, he had reason to doubt your legitimacy. He knew what your mother was like long before they became an item. I probably shouldn't mention this out of respect for your mother, but you have a right to know. With that said, it's better when a child is oblivious of their parents' faults, but your mother was a bit of a hussy. Actually, we both were at one point."

It was the last thing Drew wanted to hear, but once Patty got started, there was no stopping her. He wouldn't have guessed that Patty was a harlot back in the day or that she had a taste for younger men.

"After Miranda met your dad, she tried to change, but she couldn't get out from under Vernon. They'd sneak off and hook up when Dwight wasn't around. Mind you, he and Vernon Clevenger were best friends since grade school, at least until Dwight stopped by Vernon's place unexpectedly and caught them doing the horizontal mambo in Vernon's barn. They got in a big scuffle over her and both of them ended up with a few broken bones. Not long after that, Miranda found out that she was pregnant with you. They were married three months prior to him catching them in the act, so he figured you weren't his." Patty leaned in closer to Drew. "Between you and me, she was rationing her sexual expenditures with Dwight and gave Vernon unlimited access," Patty said and then nodded.

Drew cringed at the thought. She was right; *some things you don't want to know about your parents*.

"I guess Dwight got a swimmer in after all." Patty snickered. "You're 99.99% Dwight Tanner's son."

She picked up the glass of water and drank. Drew sat there, staring at the family photos he'd put up on the living room wall after his cleaning spell.

Without a doubt, Patty was the equivalent of a loaded forty-five that happened to be a forty-two year old woman, a handful by any stretch of the imagination. She'd unearth a crypt of secrets, airing them out after being hidden for twenty-four years.

A flood of memories came to him as he sat there; some of them were good, but most were bad. He was beyond tears at that point, but he was relieved more than anything.

"I don't like speaking ill of the dead, but—your father was an asshole," she said and drank.

"Yep, an ass kicker too."

She cackled so hard that the water she'd swallowed went down her windpipe instead. A coughing spell followed, but she managed to get a few words out after she'd finished coughing.

"And that turd, Vernon Clevenger is a vile creature, unfit to be a part of the human race."

"I second that." Drew said and huffed.

Patty finished her drink and stood up. "I should get going. I have some cleaning of my own to do."

Drew was relieved when he saw the back end of her Pontiac turning onto the blacktop. He'd learned more about his parent's now that they were dead than he did when they were alive.

The telephone rang, snapping him out of his epiphany. Drew picked up the phone. "You shouldn't have kissed me if you didn't plan on calling me in the morning."

He looked at his watch. It was almost 2 o'clock. *Damn*! "I'm sorry about that, Patty stopped by unannounced. She left a few minutes ago."

Arlene exhaled. "Anyway, Emma's spending the day with my parent's. You can come over if you like."

"I'll be there in fifteen. Uh, make that ten." He could hear Arlene snickering on the other end. "I'm leaving now."

Drew hung up and grabbed his keys and hat on the way out. During the ride there, he couldn't say if he saw a car coming or going. The only thing that mattered was getting there.

Twelve minutes later, he parked outside of her house. She stood at the top of the stairs in a thin gauzy blouse, unbuttoned down to the center of her bosom; the form of her nipples seemed to pierce the fabric, leaving little to his imagination.

As he opened the car door, Drew could hear every pulse his heart made. He walked to her, swallowing hard as his foot landed on the first step. The dark clouds gathering in the sky never crossed his mind, but he felt timid droplets of rain falling on his shoulder as he ambled up the steps.

He drew her close to him and Arlene caressed him as her lips meshed with his. Drew lifted her and she swathed her legs around his waist as he carried her through the open door with one eye closed and the other guiding him to the bedroom door.

## 32

He laid her down on the mattress, matching his body to hers, while she unbuttoned his shirt as she looked at him. Drew held the meat of her breast, lowered his head and shrouded his lips around the dark of her nipple, sucking it gently.

He'd only stimulated her nipple for a minute, however to her it felt as though his lips were still there, circling, drawing her nipple into his warm mouth, arousing her with each wave of his tongue. He pulled his shirt off, tossed it aside and hastily unbuttoned his pants, shrugged them down to his ankles, and stepped out of them.

By the time he looked up, Arlene was naked, lying on the sheets as if she was waiting for him to paint her in his version of Francisco de Goya's, "The Nude Maja." He stood there admiring her hair sprawled across the pillow, her shape, and the fine hairs covering the landscape he was angling to explore. Drew lined his body with hers, entered the warm rapturous valley between her legs and their hips clashed as he gave her his portion. Her hands kneaded the grooves of his chest as they matched each other's thrusts and troughs. Soon, melodic moans of pleasures heightened as their sexcapade reached new heights. His body shuddered as he erupted inside her and then he lay beside her.

Drew exhaled deeply as he laid there. "Are you okay? I didn't hurt you, did I?" He asked, hoping that he hadn't.

"No, you didn't." A grin spread on her face. "You were perfect." Her lips began to quiver as she looked at him. Drew eased in and kissed her.

❦ ❦ ❦

The hours that led up to dawn weren't wasted; they had ample time to explore each other's bodies before the sun rose through the mist beyond the hills that left a chill in the air. A rooster's calls roused Drew from his slumber. He looked at her nestled beside him with the thin sheet pulled up to her chest, leaving one breast exposed. He kissed her forehead and her eyes opened slightly.

"Good Morning," she said, smiling as she turned on her side.

She looked at the clock on the wall and closed her eyes, though they opened seconds later as Arlene felt him hardening against her derriere. She nudged him as he tried to put his arm around her.

In eyeshot, on the nightstand at the side of the bed was a framed photo of her husband, smiling with Arlene in his arms. She sighed, *how could I feel the way I do right now and look at that picture with a clear conscience*?

Arlene closed her eyes, aware that her actions the night before weren't of a grieving wife, but she knew that there's no timeline on grieving. After all, he'd been gone for two-and-a-half years.

She zoned out for a moment as she remembered how they'd crossed paths a few years after high school. Brian expressed interest in her, but she brushed him off. After a while, he figured the only way he could get her attention was to put it all out there. He saw her at the market one day and waited until she was outside.

'I've liked you since we were in grade school. If you're waiting on someone that you know is coming back, I'll leave you alone, but if he's not, don't waste your life on *what-if's*. I'm here. I'd like to get to know you, so at least give me a chance. I promise you won't regret it.'

*Brian was right.* She didn't regret the time they'd spent together. Despite her conflicting feelings, Arlene knew deep down that he would have wanted her to be happy. Even if it meant she'd be with someone else.

Initially, she didn't think that she'd have room in her heart for anyone else, but she didn't have to make room for Drew, he was already there ever since they were kids. She blinked her tears away. Drew rubbed the side of her upper arm. She turned, lay on her back, and tried not to look at him.

"Are you okay?" He turned her chin to him.

"Yes," she said, not wanting to spoil their time together. Arlene forced a smile and placed her head on his chest.

Drew left Arlene's home a few hours later and drove to his place. He entered his home, and noticed that the light on the answering machine was blinking. He pressed play and listened to the message: "*It's me. The wedding is next Thursday. I sent you an invitation. You haven't RSVP'd, so I thought I'd give you a call. I hope everything is okay. Give me a call when you get this message.*"

*Damn it*! He hadn't checked his voicemail in over two weeks and his mailbox for much longer than he could remember. Drew walked out to the roadside and opened the mailbox. He returned to the house with Scott's letter in hand and picked up the phone.

"Hi, I got the message and your letter. I'll be there."

"Good. I look forward to seeing you."

"I might have a guest—"

"Would that be Arlene?" Scott cut to the chase.

"Yes."

Scott's taunting laugh filled the phone line. "It's about time."

"She didn't make it easy, that's for sure," Drew said and sighed.

"Anything worth waiting for is worth fighting for. I'm happy for you. On that note, I'm going to sign off. I have to meet Brielle at the caterers to finalize the menu."

## 33

Two days before the wedding, Arlene dropped Emma off at her parent's house, picked Drew up from his place and they left for Las Vegas in her jeep.

"You aren't going to believe what I heard from my mother earlier today."

"I hope you're not expecting me to guess, because I hate guessing too. Just tell me," Drew said with a smile.

❦ ❦ ❦

After Drew had seen Wayland in town, Wayland spent the next few days drinking everything he could get his hands on, and by the end of the week he was beyond approach, crying and walking around half-naked, talking to himself. He'd been living in a makeshift shed a few miles from where he grew up. It was the closest he'd been to his parent's home since he was released from jail, and yet the two miles between them felt as though they were eons apart.

He sobered up long enough to get dressed and went for a walk. An hour later, Wayland showed up at his parent's property. Tears fell from his eyes when he saw the state of his childhood home.

The house's once white paint had for the most part stripped off the wood, leaving random scales of paint and a few strips of galvanized roof was curled back, most likely attributed to the countless wind storms that had passed through the area over the years. You wouldn't be able to tell by looking at it, but there was a time when their house had looked like a home, but after their son's went to jail, everything including the house seemed to have fallen apart.

Wayland staggered into the yard crying, hollering, "Mom! Dad!" from twenty feet away.

At that moment, Janie sprang up from the sofa, grabbed her shotgun, and came out on the front porch in a floral housedress that was buttoned down to her navel. She came out in a hurry with the wind peeling the edges of her dress back exposing her slip as she aimed the gun at him. Her thin gray hair stroked the wind as it combed through it.

"Ma! It's me."

Janie pressed the trigger and the shot landed inches from his feet.

"For Christ's sake Ma, stop shooting!"

"Don't come any closer. You better turn tail, and go back where you came from. Haven't you caused enough trouble?" Janie shouted angrily.

"I'm sorry Ma. I never meant for any of this to happen. It just got out of hand."

Wilbert, Janie's husband, heard the gunshot and ran around from the backyard. He was out of breath by the time he got around to the front. Wilbert stood there panting, with his hands on his knees.

"Janie put the gun down. No matter what you do, it's not going to bring Peter back." A stocky older man with a bald crown, wearing an oversized T-shirt and an old pair of tan dress pants pleaded with her. "It's not worth it. Put the gun down."

She dropped the gun, walked to the porch with the weight of the world on her shoulders and sat in the chair, rocking nervously as tears slipped from her eyes.

"I talked to them, but they wouldn't listen. The worst part about the mess those boys created is the fact that no matter how old your kids are, when they commit a crime the community looks at the parent's in a poor light. We never encouraged them in any of their wrong doings, but we had to deal with the shame of their actions. I know Peter was the instigator ninety-nine percent of the time, but he wouldn't do something if Wayland said no."

Wilbert sighed. "I know, but you can't hold that against him forever. Wayland lost more than we did the day Peter committed suicide. He lost a part of himself." Wilbert's eyes filled with tears. "Do you remember what they were doing when they were born?"

Janie broke down even further as she recalled, and tears came in rapid succession from her eyes. "They were holding hands. The doctor had to lift their fingers one-by-one to part them."

❦ ❦ ❦

Arlene shook her head. Drew's jaw tensed as he listened to the unsettling altercation that unfolded between Wayland and his parents.

"Anyway, after Wayland's dad calmed her down. He talked to Wayland who was still a good distance from the house."

Arlene went silent once she realized that she'd missed the exit while she was talking. She took the next one and got back on track. Drew gazed out the window as she continued.

"It turns out that Wayland had had enough of the drinking and thieving lifestyle. He wanted to go home and do something different with his life."

Drew rested his head against the chair, looked out the window and watched as the landscape slipped by.

"Peter would be proud of him. I'm hopeful that this is the first step for him to do something constructive with his life."

Arlene drove halfway and Drew took over when she was tired. He glanced in her direction, watching the lines of her hair supported on the staff of the wind. Each time he glanced at her, he felt as though his heart detached, and was floating in his chest, a strange, yet wonderful feeling. Drew smiled to himself and looked to the road ahead.

"How much longer do we have before we arrive?" Arlene asked, looking at him.

"We should be there within an hour."

"Thank goodness. This is exhausting." She reclined the passenger seat.

They arrived much later than his initial estimate, but still in plenty of time. They had a day to spare before the wedding. He hadn't gotten around to furnishing Derrick's vacant room and the laundry room wouldn't cut it with Arlene in tow. So, Scott arranged for them to stay at a nearby hotel.

Drew swung by Scott's place before going to the hotel. He looked at the countdown display as they rode the elevator to their floor.

"I think you'll like them, they're a fascinating bunch."

The elevator parted and they stepped out. They moseyed down the hall to the apartment door, and knocked. Scott stood in the doorway as it opened.

"Come in. I'm glad you could make it. How was the drive?" Scott opened his arms.

"Not too bad. We took turns." Drew hugged him. "I'd like you to meet my *girlfriend*, Arlene McQuillen." Drew's face lit up.

"It's nice to meet you," they each said as she went down the line shaking their hands.

"We've heard so much about you," Lou said.

"It's nice to meet you too. I feel like I know you all. I've heard so many good things about you," she said and smiled.

"He was lying to you then," Lou said.

Derrick and Scott broke out in laughter. Drew and Arlene joined in seconds later.

"I can see why Drew was losing his senses over you. You're easy on the eyes." Lou tapped Drew on the shoulder and Drew nudged him with his elbow.

"Thank you," Arlene said, blushing.

"We've had a long drive so we won't stay long. I just wanted to stop by before we meet up later," Drew said.

❦ ❦ ❦

They left shortly after and drove to the hotel. Arlene got a few hours of sleep before she woke later that evening.

"Shouldn't you be getting ready for the party?" Drew asked. Brielle's back-up singer's planned a bachelorette party and Arlene got an invite.

"Yes, but I'm not sure if I should go or not. Besides, I don't know anyone there, which could prove to be an awkward situation."

"You do have a point, but she was kind enough to invite you, so it would be nice if you can make it, but I'm leaving that up to you."

Arlene sat there for a while musing over the situation. "I'll go, but if I feel uncomfortable, I'll leave."

233

"Okay, as long as you're doing it because you want to and not because you feel pressured in any way."

"Trust me; nobody can make me do anything that I don't want to." Arlene swished her hair and put her hand on her hip.

Drew smiled as he looked at her. She hadn't lost her bite after all. The feisty, daring Arlene that he admired for most of his life was still in there somewhere just waiting for someone to piss her off.

"I should go and get ready."

A car picked her up an hour later and dropped her off at the party's venue. Arlene smiled as she looked up at Chip's Hunks blinking sign. She stepped out of the cab and entered the club.

Soothing music streamed from the speakers stationed around the dimly lit room. Thin white fabric hung from decorative columns and at the far left of the stage was a table filled with hors d'oeuvres. Everyone in the room was dressed in roman attire—even the waiters.

Arlene stood near the bar while Brielle looked over her shoulder from where she sat at a table near the door.

She glanced at the picture Scott sent via her phone and approached Arlene.

"Hi, I'm Scott's fiancé, Brielle," she said close to her ear.

"It's nice to meet you."

"Likewise, I'm glad you're here. As you can see, we're all dressed in Roman garb, but don't worry, you won't be out of sync for long. We have a selection of costumes in the dressing room for you to choose from."

Arlene smiled. "That sounds like fun. Lead the way." Arlene followed Brielle into the changing room.

Sometime later, she emerged in a draped, white, goddess, open-back dress with a gold sash at the waist and bust area.

"You can sit at my table or where ever you like," Brielle suggested.

"I'll sit with you." Arlene focused on the stage area, designed to look like the arena of a coliseum.

🐛 🐛 🐛

DJ Tryst switched the music from classic Pop to modern club music for a while until his mouth moved closer to the microphone. "Ladies, I hope you're enjoying yourselves thus far. Per your request, we have gladiators battling for your affection and *tips* tonight. Let's show Asian Persuasion some love." DJ Tryst's deep, sultry voice competed with the applause and whistles that erupted in the room.

Asian Persuasion emerged in the spotlight with a bronze helmet lined with red feathers in a Mohawk at the center, baring his naked chest and broad shoulders that were covered by bronze armguards. A studded war belt, adorned with strips of leather attached to his skirt, swayed as "Magic Man" by Heart played.

A catchy guitar solo meshed with a drumbeat cut through the area like a thin blade, energizing the crowd. He grasped the pole at the center of the stage, inverted his body, and rotated his splayed muscular legs like a propeller until his feet touched the floor. Many clapped their hands over the head, including Arlene, who also swayed to the beat.

Asian Persuasion ran his hand along the oiled crevices of his eight-pack and motioned into a sliding step to the side as he rippled his body, flexing his arms, swiveling his hips, while he closed the gap between him and the crowd. He skimmed the front row for a willing participant and reached for Leslie, Brielle's back-up singer's hand, and she strutted on the stage adorned in a white draped skort, a cream leather bustier embellished with gold hugging her upper torso, and gold stiletto boots. Her natural honey-brown complexion glistened under the stage lights as her dark-brown hair rested on her shoulders.

Mesmerized by her beauty, he danced only for her at that point, while she ran her hands on his chest with her back to the crowd. Asian Persuasion took off his belt, tossed it aside, and unpinned his man-skirt, doing so while he made his chest quiver. A lengthy guitar solo followed that brought the crowd to their feet.

He picked her up, and she wrapped her legs around his waist while he snaked his body down to the floor, and gyrated his center an inch above her. Bills rained onto the stage from every direction as he role-played with Leslie on the floor.

By the end of his dance, Arlene leaned into Brielle. "This has been a fabulous experience, but I'm going back to the hotel."

"Aww, so soon? The party's just getting started."

"I'm afraid so. The ride to Las Vegas was tiring and I only got three hours of sleep." Arlene eased her chair away from the table.

"I understand. Thanks for coming." Brielle hugged her. Arlene sent Drew a message as she went to the dressing room. She changed and walked out to the entrance.

❦ ❦ ❦

Meanwhile, Drew, Scott, and Derrick were a few blocks from the club eating dinner at a Mediterranean restaurant.

"I hope Arlene didn't have too much fun. I can't compete with those guys," Drew said and drank some of his champagne.

"I wouldn't worry about that, if I were you. Some women like to watch men strip, but I could probably count on one hand those who would take them home to meet their parents. I was fortunate that Brielle saw past what I did for a living and took the time to get to know me as a person instead of a sex object," he said and then nodded. "Thankfully, my days of strangers pawing my

238

bare flesh are over. I've had enough of that to last a lifetime. At this point in my life, I've decided to devote my passions elsewhere. Actually, I have some exciting news to share with you guys."

"I'm dying to know what it is?" Derrick asked.

"I've always dreamed of starting a program to help disadvantaged teens. Thanks to my hard work and diligence, I've been able to do just that. As of last week, I started an outreach program for teenagers in foster care."

"That's great. I'm proud of you. Mom would be too," Derrick said as his eyes moistened.

"This is right up your alley," Drew said and then nodded. "You're doing something meaningful. How did you do it?"

"It took a few months to line things up, but I recruited successful business owners to act as mentors that were once in the foster care system. They are paired with a teen and their mentee becomes an intern in the mentor's company, gaining life skills that will aid them in becoming productive citizens. Mentors also visits the teen's home that they're assigned to, take them on field trips and, at the end of the program, they receive a stipend for their first two years of college."

Derrick nodded as he listened to his brother's master plan. "I knew you had a big heart, but you just took my respect for you to a whole other level. When I grow up, I want to be like you."

Scott smiled. "I appreciate the love, but don't be like me, always strive to be better." Scott paid the bill and they walked to the exit.

Drew's phone beeped. He checked his message just as they were about to flag a cab. They got in and had the driver swing by the club to get Arlene.

They picked her up and pulled away from the club. On the way back to the hotel, Arlene took in the scenery of the strip's busy nightlife.

"Dinner was great. Thanks for the invite."

"You're welcome. I hope you had a good time at the bachelorette party," Scott said.

"It was an enjoyable experience," she said blushing.

Within a matter of ten to fifteen minutes, they arrived at the hotel.

"Good night, see you tomorrow," Drew said and the cab moved away from the curb as they entered the hotel.

Scott and Brielle's wedding took place the following day. It was an elaborate affair held at the MGM Grand Hotel & Casino with two hundred of their closest friends as witnesses. They stood in front a wall of roses as the pastor expressed the importance of family and marriage.

Scott looked debonair in his Ralph Lauren classic fitted suit and Brielle exuded old world elegance in an off-the-shoulder vintage Steve McQueen pearl-white gown. Derrick stood at Scott's side as his best man as they read the vows they'd prepared, and by the time they were through, just about everyone in the room was emotional.

The celebration continued with a reception at the same venue. Mr. and Mrs. Scott Derwin made their toast and ventured out on the dance floor for their first dance as husband and wife, which amounted to them doing a choreographed spoof of the song, "Moves Like

Jagger" by Maroon Five. Everyone in the attendance was thoroughly amused.

After their dance, everyone else joined them on the dance floor. Scott saw the faces of his roommates in the crowd every now and then. They all seemed to be enjoying themselves, especially Lou Chang, who was smiling from ear to ear with Leslie close to his hip.

Outside of work, Scott had never seen him with anyone. All he seemed to focus on was getting to that number one spot, but by the looks of it, Lou was enamored by Leslie. Maybe there was hope for him after all.

Once the dancing died down, the newlyweds endured countless introductions and engaged in small talk before Scott lifted Brielle and carried her into the waiting limousine as the guests tossed rice their way. They left the reception and drove to the airport to catch their flight.

❦ ❦ ❦

Drew and Arlene left the reception shortly after the bride and groom left. She fell asleep before they made it to the hotel. When they got there, he carried her up to their room, but wondered how a petite woman like Arlene could be so heavy. Drew was relieved once he laid her on the bed. He kept his eyes open long enough to undress, lay down and fell asleep.

Hours later, the obnoxious blare of the alarm clock interrupted the silence in the room, waking them. They wakened feeling more exhausted than when they'd initially fallen asleep, but they had another long trip ahead of them, so they prepared to leave and stopped by the hotel's cafeteria on the way out.

Shortly after they'd left, they were driving on the interstate back to Alabaster, engaging in light conversation and singing songs streaming from the radio, but it got annoying after singing three songs back-to-back. Drew drove nonstop for five hours after taking the wheel from Arlene, and it seemed like forever before they finally passed the Welcome to Alabaster sign.

It was almost dinnertime by then. On the way home, they stopped at a drive-thru, bought a bucket of chicken, and ate some on their way to her parent's house. She checked up on Emma even though she didn't have to pick her up until the following day and then they drove to his place.

There was a chill in the air when they stepped out into the night and strolled to the front door.

"Would you like to go for a walk?" He asked, holding her hand.

"Sure, why not."

"I'll get a blanket, it's a bit cold."

He opened the front door, grabbed a blanket from the sofa, and came out on the porch. They strolled to the pond where they first met as kids. They sat down with their backs against the trunk of a tree, looking out at the pond. Arlene wrapped the blanket around their shoulders as they looked up at the constellations.

"Do you know what became of Muffin?" Drew asked. "I never got around to asking Dwight."

Arlene pressed her lips inward and sighed. "I took Muffin with me after I learned that you weren't coming back. He was a sweet dog. I couldn't leave him with that curmudgeon. Muffin was the only part of you that I had left." She didn't say anything for a few minutes. "He stayed with us until he passed away three years ago. He's buried in my backyard." Arlene wiped her tears. "Every time Muffin heard a car or someone walked in the yard, he'd perk up and then he would lower his head. I think he was waiting for you. Actually, we both were at one point."

Drew's eyes moistened. "He probably was. I feel bad about that, but I think deep down he understood." Drew exhaled. "I'm glad you two had each other. Dwight would have probably let him starve to death."

"I wouldn't put it past him," Arlene said.

They gazed at the crescent moon coming into view as a thin band of clouds released it, allowing it to light the heavens.

"It's been a while since I've been out here." Drew gazed at the dark body of water before them.

"The last time I was here was when you left town." Arlene looked at him. Drew put his hand to her cheek and rubbed it gently as he looked at her.

"I remember the first time I saw your reflection on this pond. I thought you were the prettiest girl I'd ever seen."

She snuggled closer to him. "I thought you were fetching."

"Fetching… what's that supposed to mean?" Drew asked, raising his brow.

Arlene smirked. "I thought you were handsome." She gazed at him tenderly. "Promise me something." She held his hand.

Drew smiled at her. "It depends on what it is." He rested the back of his head against the tree.

"Promise me that you won't leave the way you did before."

"I promise. I'm not going anywhere without you ever again." Drew eased in and kissed her.

www.ingramcontent.com/pod-product-compliance
Lightning Source LLC
Chambersburg PA
CBHW020321200626
46814CB00006BB/2347